American Survivor

American Apocalypse

Book I

By

AJ Newman

*

This book is dedicated to Patsy, my beautiful wife of thirty-four years, who assists with everything from Beta reading to censor duties. She enables me to write, golf, and enjoy my life with her and our mob of Shih Tzu's.

Thanks to Cliff at Mustang Publishing LLC, my editor for improving my work and correcting any ammunition and weapon oops. Thanks to Wes, David, and Mitchell who are Beta readers for my novels. They gave many suggestions that helped improve my novel.

Thanks again to the state of Oregon for being such an excellent setting for this story. I thoroughly enjoyed my research trip to Oregon to visit Bandon, Ashland, Medford, Grants Pass, and all of the bergs and land between them. That area is the setting for this story and several of my other novels.

AJ Newman

*

Published by Newalk LLC.

Owensboro, Kentucky

*

Books by AJ Newman

American Apocalypse:

American Survivor   Descent Into Darkness (Spring 2018)

Alien Apocalypse: The Virus   Surviving

A Family's Apocalypse Series: Cities on Fire – Family Survival

After the Solar Flare - a Post-Apocalyptic series:

Alone in the Apocalypse   Adventures in the Apocalypse*

The Day America Died series:

New Beginnings   Old Enemies   Frozen Apocalypse

"The Adventures of John Harris" - a Post-Apocalyptic America series:

Surviving   Hell in the Homeland   Tyranny in the Homeland
Revenge in the Homeland...Apocalypse in the Homeland   John Returns

"A Samantha Jones Murder Mystery Thriller series:

Where the Girls Are Buried   Who Killed the Girls?

Books by AJ Newman and Cliff Deane

Terror in the USA: Virus: Strain of Islam

These books are available on Amazon:

http://www.amazon.com/-/e/B00HT84V6U

To contact the Author, please leave comments @:
www.facebook.com/newmananthonyj

☆

Please read Mack Norman and my novel "Rogues Origin." I highly recommend the series, "Rogues Apocalypse.

Rogues Origin tells the story of how some unique people survive and prosper during an apocalypse caused by a nuclear EMP attack on the USA and the rest of the world. These people are unique because they quickly decide to do what it takes to survive before everything falls entirely apart. The main characters are a Post-Apocalyptic Science Fiction writer, a crooked Federal Marshal, an NYPD Policeman, a Mobster, and a woman who is a mob enforcer.

What would you do if you knew you had a few hours before the shit hit the fan. These people take action and fight back against the apocalypse.

BOOKS BY
AJ NEWMAN
&
MACK NORMAN

Rogues Apocalypse Series:
Rogues Origin
Rogues Rising
Rogues Journey

Mack's books are available on Amazon @

https://www.amazon.com/Mack-Norman/e/B0779JZWC4/ref=dp_byline_cont_ebooks_1

-

American Survivor

By

AJ Newman

☆

Chapter 1 Prelude

This is a post apocalyptic survival story about Joe Harp who is just an ordinary man. He was an overweight mechanic living in Tennessee who didn't care about politics or what happened outside of the USA. He had never been in the military and had never been a prepper or doomsday nut. He knew how to camp, hunt and fish but not much else. He had recently lost his fiancee and best friend. His Grandmother, who he was devoted to, had also recently died. Just when his world had fallen apart, it really falls apart; TEOTWAWKI (the end of the world as we know it) hits the fan. Now he has to scramble to survive in the Oregon woods after China and North Korea conduct a two-pronged financial and then an EMP attack on the USA.

An Apocalypse is coming to a neighborhood near you. The only questions are - When will it happen, and what will be the cause of devastation catastrophic enough to cause an Apocalypse? Most people don't have military training, and are not Preppers; so what is the likely scenario they will face, when TSHTF (the shit hits the fan)? Joe has to face these same challenges. The answers are:

1. Food shortages – Stores will be empty in three days. They won't be restocked, and farmers will be fighting for their lives as starving hordes from the cities descend upon them.

2. Water shortages – There will be water, but it will need to be purified. Your faucet will go dry in a few days.

3. Power shortages – The grid will be down if it's a nuclear EMP (Electromagnetic Pulse) attack or Coronal Mass Ejection event (huge solar flare). If the grid is not destroyed, most workers will still go home to protect their families.

4. Medicine – Factories will shut down, and none will be produced. Many people will die during the first 90 days.

5. Law Enforcement – Most police will go home to protect their families. Criminals will not be kept in check. Crime will soar.

6. Transportation – An EMP attack or CME could fry all electronics, and your car has computers. You will be walking. Trucks won't move goods to the stores from the numerous warehouses.

So, my last question to you is – Will you be like Joe and fight to become the American Survivor or will you crawl into a hole and die? Your choice. I will fight like Joe does.

AJ Newman

☆

Chapter 2

The end of the world started a month before the actual events that caused the apocalypse. The events that led up to the apocalypse appeared the same as a thousand other events that occur daily. A cyber-attack, China threatening Taiwan, Rocket Man threatening to nuke the USA and you know the rest of the large list. The point is that most average citizens were fatigued by the constant barrage of doomsday news and didn't key on the actual events that were the warning signs to prepare for doomsday.

February 21, 2038, was the day that Joe found out his best friend for life had been seeing his fiancee, Gwen, and the bad news was Joe couldn't thank the unlucky bastard. Later that week his beloved Grandma died, and the world ended, as he knew it. His Grandma dying was a tragedy but turned out to be a bit of good news for Joe. The world ending as he knew it was a bad thing for Joe and much worse for most of the rest of the world. Joe was just an auto mechanic and regular guy without any military training. He had never been a prepper type. He was an unlikely candidate to survive the apocalypse, but here I am telling you about his adventures many years later.

Now back to the girlfriend and best friend. (I'll get to Grandma in good time.) Not only were the two caught with their pants down, but they were also the two unluckiest lovebirds in the world. Both were buck naked in the back of Joe's Explorer in a thunderstorm, with the back seat folded down doing what lovers do in the back seat of a car. The storm raged as the two made love passionately without regard to the storm or anything else. Unfortunately, a huge tree toppled over, crushed the SUV, and pinned their naked bodies together in death a week before Gwen and Joe's wedding.

The State Police ran the plate, found Joe's name, and went to see his next of kin. They went to his mom's home to break the bad news to her and his dad about Joe's death. Thank God, Joe was sitting there when she was told he was dead, or the poor women would have suffered a stroke. The rest of that part of the story went downhill quickly as the Trooper took Joe to the scene of the disaster to ID the victims. The roof was crushed down so only Darren's head, and shoulder could be seen until the rescue crew used the Jaws of Life to extract both bodies.

It took Joe a minute for the light to switch on in his head, but Joe began thanking God that his best friend had stolen her away from him. Then he kicked his dead friend's body for sneaking behind his back when he would have gladly given Gwen to him. Joe had been tired of her bossy, manipulative ways for some time before the accident. She expected Joe to jump when she snapped her fingers. He didn't miss her at all but was sorry they died even though he couldn't help but laugh.

Joe Harp was 30 years old, five feet ten inches tall, and 220 pounds when his world went to crap. He had blue eyes and brown hair. He was a good-looking man although a bit overweight from too much junk food, beer, and pizzas. Joe didn't care about politics and was a very nice guy who would help anyone in need. He hated college but his girlfriend pushed him to go, and he was a lackluster student. He cracked jokes and loved to pull pranks on his fellow workers. He always had a smile on his face before the apocalypse.

Joe wasn't into watching sports on TV and was never personally involved in sports after he graduated from high school. He lived alone in an apartment in Smyrna, Tennessee close to the golf course. He spent his free time camping, fishing, hunting, and playing golf. He didn't think golf was a sport since he was able to ride in a cart and drink beer with his buddies. He was free except when his longtime girlfriend, Gwen, didn't have plans for him to jump through some new hoop for her snotty friends. She was trying to add culture to Joe's life without much success. Joe did pretty much whatever she said just to keep her happy. A common phrase heard from Joe was, "Yes dear," to avoid an argument.

They had been together since they were juniors in high school and Gwen was the ambitious one of the two. She attended Middle Tennessee State University and earned her Master's degree in Computer Science from Vanderbilt. She had a high paying job at a bank in downtown Nashville and wanted Joe to move there when they were married. She never paid attention to his protests and knew he'd do whatever she asked. She had changed over the years while Joe remained the same good old boy from Tennessee that loved fixing cars. She had recently become ashamed of what she considered his lowly mechanic's job.

Gwen wanted a large wedding even though her parents were from a modest background and had to take out a second mortgage on their home. Gwen had been so wrapped up in her own success and ambition she didn't notice that she had left Joe behind her. One day she told Joe what changes he had to make in his life and was shocked when he sat her down and said no to every one of her demands. Joe's "Yes, dear," days were over.

Gwen realized the wedding was a mistake over wine with Joe's best friend the night of the storm. He worked in the same building where Gwen worked, and they soon became very close. They shared many of the same beliefs and ambitions. They kept their secret from Joe until the tree fell and crushed their world.

Joe took a couple of days off from the Ford Dealership, where he worked as the lead mechanic, in Murfreesboro, Tennessee. He stayed home grieving the loss of his best friend and thanking God, he hadn't married Gwen. He tried to act as if he was grieving for Gwen but figured she was already bossing everyone around up there and possibly down there.

Joe was one of the good guys and always helped his friends and even strangers. His dark brown hair was in contrast to his blue eyes and fair skinned complexion. His face turned red too quickly to suit him, and he always had a smile on his face. He was overweight, and Gwen often got after him about overeating junk food and pizza along with his favorite beer. Joe had laughed it off and told her to find a skinny guy because he loved his pizza and beer. After seeing Darren and her in the wreck, he felt she must have taken his advice. Darren was six feet tall and weighed 175 pounds while Joe was 5'10" and weighed 210 pounds.

Joe knew people were laughing behind his back, and he expected memes of their naked butts to be on Facebook any day. He didn't give a care about Gwen but didn't like being the butt of the jokes. Then a real tragedy occurred that had a silver lining and a second disaster that killed billions of people.

Joe was out on his patio drinking too much of his favorite IPA while stuffing his mouth with pizza celebrating his freedom when his music stopped, and the announcer mentioned something about a potential cyber-attack overseas. Joe changed the channel to another country music station and grabbed an ice cold beer. The IPA bit his tongue as he downed a mouthful and tickled his nose. He heard a noise from his driveway, and his dad drove up and parked.

"Dad, have a beer."

"Not now son, your Grandma has passed away in her sleep at Aunt Jane's home."

"Oh, shit. I'm so sorry. I loved her and will miss her a lot. Dad, I know you were closer to Grandma than I was but I will miss her very much. Her quick wit and ball busting my cousins and your sisters made my day at every family event."

"Yes, she was a character, but you are wrong. You and mom were much closer than she and I ever were. I spent too much time rebelling against her and her way of doing things. She doted on you and took a much softer approach with you. You should have been raised in her house. She kept things lively and would bust your ass in a skinny minute if you broke the rules, but she would also stand up for us kids when we needed it the most," his Dad said with tears in his eyes.

"Dad, we need to celebrate. Grandma wasn't someone to want people to sit around moping. She would want something like an Irish wake. Have a beer," Joe said.

Grandma had been 97 but was very active up to the day of her death. Joe had been very close to her since he was young and still called her every week to see how she was doing. She had taken him for long hikes in the Oregon woods on their property and paid for the plane tickets to fly him out for a month every spring when he was in high school to help her around the ranch. She paid Joe to help tend the cabins in the woods east of Ashland and to cut weeds and trees down to keep the area around the three cabins cleared.

Joe's Grandpa had died when Joe was nine years old, so he didn't remember much about him. He dimly remembered the walks in the woods that his Grandpa had called, *digging for treasure*. His Grandpa had always stuck something in the hole instead of taking anything out. Grandpa had made a fortune in lumber, and before he died, they owned one of the largest sawmills in the state, plus several large tracts of land with cabins and houses.

Grandma taught Joe about hunting, fishing, and hiking from an early age until Joe got out of college and was busy working. He only saw her for a few days each year at holidays or funerals but never missed calling her and talking for hours.

Sometimes she would rant about politics and how the world was going to hell in a hand basket or give Joe tips on which stock to purchase. She always sent him one share of her latest hot stock for Christmas, and he still had every one of them.

Joe didn't go to his fiancee's funeral but forced himself to go to his friend's funeral, before flying out to Oregon with his parents for his Grandma's funeral. His Grandma's funeral went as planned; however, his greedy assed relatives were salivating over Grandma's money and land. His cousins were on the internet ordering fancy trucks and sports cars, but he and his parents only wanted Grandma back.

That afternoon Joe and his dad went to the liquor store and brought back enough beer, wine, and liquor for a small army. They invited everyone back to Aunt Jane's home for a celebration of his Grandma's life. Aunt Becky and her wimpy husband thought they were insulting her mom's memory. They apparently didn't know Agnes Pearl White very well because she would be cracking a joke and drinking heartily.

This was just what Joe needed to get back on track.

The next day the lawyer read Grandma's will, and there were a bunch of pissed off people because the local animal shelter, Aunt Jane, Joe's parents, and Joe were the only ones who received anything from Grandma. Joe received $30,000 and a large tract of land a few miles east of Ashland, Oregon.

Joe was dumbfounded. He was starting to offer to split the money and land with the others when his dad said, "Joe, you were the only grandchild that had contacted Grandma in the last five years, and the others only saw her on the holidays.

You deserve the land and money. Hell, mom gave the animal shelter over a million dollars."

Later, Grandma's lawyer asked, "Joe could you join me in the conference room. Your Grandmother was a wealthy and very opinionated lady. I knew her for over 40 years, and she loved you more than I can say. She left instructions to meet with you in private to give you this letter which explains the items on my desk.

The letter read:

Dear Joe:

As they say, if you are reading this, then I am dead. I had cancer that had metastasized, and Doc gave me about six months to live. I didn't tell anyone because I'm 97 years old and that's long enough. My only regret is that we won't have our weekly phone calls, but so you don't miss me I took some of my last days on Earth to write 134 letters to you that give you more of my wit, wisdom, and charm. Read one every week, and we will be able to continue our weekly chats. I hope you decide to stay and live on the property. I have loved and cherished that land for over fifty years. I have also added clues to enable you to find the most valuable treasure on this Earth. I have left my maps of the land and all of my favorite places on your property.

I only left you a small amount of money because I want you to struggle a bit as you make your way through life. Your Grandpa and I were broke many times during our marriage, and those were the times that brought us closer. You and your woman, when you get one, need the same opportunity.

Now for some advice. Never confuse lust with love. Sow your wild oats but never screw anything that can't be unscrewed. Don't marry a girl until you can't stand to live without her. Last my favorite. Never eat the yellow snow.

You should be around 30 years old and should have a great life ahead of you. The stock I sent you over the years is worth a small fortune but never sell it. Save it to pass on to Joe Jr. I left you money, and now you have the thing that, other than you, that I hold most dear: my land.

PS There are five letters that you need to read this week. They are in the front of the book.

I will be watching from above. Live a good life, and I know you'll make me prouder of you than I already am!

Love Grandma.

Joe laughed several times as he read the letter and had tears flowing from his eyes by the end. On the table was a large three-ring binder with plastic pages that contained three sealed envelopes per side for a total of 134 letters and several paper maps. There were 30 letters to be opened one per day and then one per week afterward. A cover letter for the maps had in large letters, *"Joe, your GPS doesn't have the good stuff on it. You will need to use my maps with my hand printed notes to find my treasure or should I say your treasure."*

Joe read the first letter. *"Joe, now the fun begins. Go to the Outfitter store and purchase the items on the list below before you go to the property.*

Love Grandma.

Joe took a gander at the list and saw several guns, ammo, a folding shovel, and lots of camping gear.

Joe's dad and mom wanted him to go back home with them, but Joe was excited to go out and see his property, "Dad, I sat on my patio a week ago trying to decide if I should celebrate or be sad my two best friends were dead. Now I have land and some money out here in the woods of Oregon."

"Son, do what you have to do, but where will you live?"

"I haven't been out to this tract of land in years, but I'll never forget the main cabin that Grandpa built. Remember he was one of those people who thought the Russians were going to nuke us back in the day and wanted the cabin to be his retreat. I hope Grandma kept it and the other cabins up."

"Okay son, I'll go through your things and ship the items on your list to you next week. I guess the good news is now I'll have a place to go hunting with you."

"Dad, we both love hunting but haven't been in years, but I remember like it was yesterday the camping trips we took nearly every weekend; oh, yeah let's not forget that weekend you made me camp by myself to get ready for my Boy Scout Order of the Arrow. Then how you made me skin and prepare the game, we hunted. You know what, Dad, I loved that time of my life, and thanks to you and Grandpa, I know I can make it up there on my own, Hell, I prefer my own company to 'bout anybody, 'cept you, mom, and Grandma. Hey, Dad, I'll bet you a dollar that I lose this extra weight I'm carryin' around, too.

I'm going to spend a little money on hunting gear and live off the land. I'll even grow my own food and raise some animals. Come on out when you can, and we'll have a great time."

Joe took his mom and dad to the airport and then drove to the Ford Dealer in Ashland to buy a used 4x4 to help him get around.

"You work for Ford in Murfreesboro. I can get you a squeal of a deal on a new F150," the salesman said.

"I want that old 1975 Bronco on the back lot. The mechanic said it was in perfect running condition and has new tires. It will do fine to get back to Ashland every once in a while," Joe pushed back.

"Just trying to help."

The Bronco was black with a black rag top and soft full doors. It had a black interior and all the four wheeling goodies. It had a winch on the front bumper, and a handyman jack attached to the back beside a jerry can for gasoline. The tires were 35 inches, had massive lugs, and would go through any snow unless it high centered.

Joe sat at the salesman's desk while the salesman acted like he was trying to get Joe a good deal. There was a radio on the desk playing old '80s music when abruptly a newswoman said, "The Chinese have moved their aircraft Carrier Group closer to Taiwan, and the NSA reports the Chinese have moved several divisions of their crack troops to staging areas where their amphibious ships are located. Our President has ordered two more of our Carrier Groups to the area. We will keep you posted on any significant events."

Joe ignored the announcer and read a hot rod magazine. Joe agreed to the price, and they signed the documents. He now had a Bronco.

The salesman told him about a place that had several used trailers, so Joe paid for the Bronco and headed out to find a trailer and purchase supplies. He bought a suitable trailer and then went to Cobb's Outfitters and Outdoors Store in Ashland to purchase a few guns, ammunition, animal traps, and a long list of other items he thought he would need to live off the land.

He walked up to the camping section, where a man and the female department manager were having a heated discussion. "Mrs. Simms, I'm sorry you are being evicted, but I'm just the messenger," the man said.

Cobie Simms answered with tears in her eyes. "But where will my daughter and I live? Everything is too expensive in Ashland, and most won't take my daughter's dog. Why is the building being torn down?"

She then quoted various laws and regulations, but the man replied, "Lady, some rich jerk from California bought several buildings and is tearing them down to build nicer homes that will sell for millions. Look, you received notice 60 days ago and have to be out today. These guys have a dozen lawyers on retainer. Good luck."

"But I can't take off work. I'll lose my job." Tears flowed down her cheek as Cobie glared at the man.

The man ended the confrontation with, "Mrs. Connie M. Simms, the sheriff will be at your apartment at 3:00 pm today. Watch my men place your possessions out on the lawn for you to remove."

The short, feisty lady said, "That's Ms. Simms."

Joe watched as the beautiful lady's cheeks turned red and her voice cracked as she tried to keep her composure. Joe felt sorry for the attractive raven-haired beauty but went on with his shopping and minded his own business. After the betrayal by his fiancee, Joe didn't have much sympathy for any woman in trouble, but the tears tugged at his heartstrings as he forced himself to walk away from her. As he walked away, he thought that the woman seemed very familiar. She was sharp-tongued, opinionated, and brilliant. He felt his Grandma would have said, "Boy that gal is built like a brick shithouse."

He thought about this woman on and off the rest of the day while getting everything ready for his trip to the land.

Joe had almost finished his shopping when he walked past the archery department, tried out several compound bows, and decided to buy one. He hadn't hunted with a bow since he was a Boy Scout. It seemed like a good idea, so he purchased the bow, arrows, and the accessories recommended by the sales clerk.

Joe was becoming more and more excited about returning to a life he had trained for as a child. He knew his weight would return to what, for him, would be normal.

Joe parked the Bronco and trailer in front of his motel room, checked the lock on the door to the trailer, and went to his room for the night. He turned on the news and took a shower. He lay down on the bed as the TV announcer said, "We have breaking news out of Taiwan. The entire Taiwanese financial banking system has been the subject of a cyber attack. Markets around the world are in chaos. Taiwanese officials are certain the Chinese military is responsible. Taiwan has threatened nuclear retaliation if the Chinese move troops toward them.

President Jackson has deployed two aircraft carrier groups to the area to assist Taiwan if this should become a shooting war. Jackson has warned the Chinese not to make any hostile moves against Taiwan."

Joe fell asleep with only his new property on his mind. He wasn't going to waste his time worrying about people ten thousand miles away.

Joe spent the next two days in lawyer's offices and banks getting his inheritance handled and all of the transfers and paperwork completed. He took the time to read another letter from his Grandma. The letter read:

Dear Joe:

To help you I have added an alphabetized list of problems, and heartaches at the end of the book that refers to the letter with my advice on the subject. I thought of this when you gave me the advice to play nice with all of my kids and grandkids. Well crap, I didn't listen to your advice and didn't provide the others with a damned thing, which is what they deserved. So remember, I will give you advice, but you don't have to take it.

Love Grandma.

The next morning Joe picked up a few groceries and drove out of Ashland on Dead Indian Highway. After about two miles, he turned right on an unmarked road that wound past several companies and continued into the hills. He began to see patches of snow on the side of the road and around the base of trees in the woods. The snow steadily built up as he went higher into the mountains.

Joe hadn't seen the property since his Grandma broke her hip when he was in his senior year of college. He didn't recognize anything along the way. He pulled out his Grandma's map of the property and some old aerial photographs that showed several structures on the property. He followed the route out of Ashland to where an x on the map was located. Joe found himself in a meadow with nothing but grass surrounded by trees. The x had a note that said, "Start here, Joe."

The air was crisp and had a bite to it as Joe took a deep breath and coughed. The scent of Pine was strong, but the air also had a slight earthy smell. Joe put a warm parka on because it was freezing this high up on the mountainside. His ears were cold, and his nose was running as he dressed in the warm clothes. He strapped on his heavy backpack and his new Ruger .44 Magnum revolver. He headed out, walked around the property and followed the map to find his cabin. He had purchased the big bore pistol and all of the other gear because Grandma had warned him about bears and mountain lions roaming the hills. He also had a .308 hunting rifle, .22 Ruger 10/22, and a Ruger MKIV, so he was set up for hunting large and small game. While Joe didn't give a crap about politics, he was very happy that Congress passed the universal gun laws back in 2021 or he would have had to wait to become a resident of Oregon to purchase pistols.

He took a last look at the contents of the large envelope and pulled out the deed to the land, which had some fine print on the bottom right corner. The fine print made Joe's jaw drop when he saw his tract of land was 1,107.3 acres. He read the entire description several times and looked around but couldn't see the three structures mentioned in the paperwork. He looked at Google Earth on his tablet and saw several dirt paths winding through the property, so he headed to the far end of the fifty-yard broad meadow to find the path.

The path was overgrown, and briars tugged at his pants leg. The snow was a few inches deep, as he headed east up a hillside to where the main cabin should be located. The trail was steep, and it brought back memories of when he and his Grandma had walked to the top years ago to get to the cabin. The walks came back to him but left him confused. He should have seen the cabin by now. He was a bit worried that he saw several tire tracks in the snow crossing his property. The tracks traveled across the southern end of his land and went southwest. He wondered if hunters were poaching on his land, and thought he should purchase no hunting or trespassing signs on his next trip into town.

He stared at the woods, but only saw pine trees, so he walked fifty feet further on up the hill. He still didn't see anything but pine trees and overgrown bushes. He was frustrated now and thought that perhaps the cabin had burned down, but then he remembered that it had a large basement below it that couldn't have disappeared. He walked a few steps more and caught a glimpse of something odd. He walked toward the object. The cabin was only twenty feet from him, and the strange object was the steps up to the porch.

The outside of the cabin was in good shape, but weeds and trees had overgrown the front yard making it hard to see until one bumped into it. Joe liked the natural camouflage. He decided to clear only the weeds closest to the cabin and cut only a few limbs that brushed against the metal roof.

The inside of the cabin was covered in dust and smelled that musty, stale aroma that left a bad taste in your mouth. The pieces of furniture had dusty white sheets covering them. The living room had a massive fireplace with iron pots hanging from iron hooks. They had been used to cook stews and boil water for years. There was a faint smell of burned wood coming from the hearth.

The bedrooms had furniture from the mid-1900's and hardly showed any wear. The bedroom closet had sheets, pillowcases, and blankets stored in plastic bags. The cabin was dusty and had a few cobwebs but otherwise was mostly ready for him to move into.

He dropped his pack on the couch, explored each room, and then went downstairs to the basement. There was very little light in the basement, so he fetched his LED lantern to explore the basement, which had been broken up into several rooms. One room had shelves stacked with food of all kinds. He opened a couple of the home-canned beans and tomatoes, and his nose was assaulted by the pungent sulfur smell. Had he looked closer he would have seen the bacteria growths in the jars. Most of the food had to be pitched because it was very old, but there were a few boxes of sealed survival food that had years of shelf life left.

The other rooms had tools, camping gear, and large boxes of unknown contents. The final room Joe explored had a thick steel door. Behind it was a small apartment. The walls were covered with more shelves containing thousands of books. Joe hadn't had a book in his hands in years. He'd had his first tablet at four years old. He looked at the titles. There was a mixture of fiction and every topic from how to field dress a deer to how to make furniture by hand. He also found a whole section on how to survive the apocalypse.

He had purchased cleaning supplies expecting to have to clean the place up but now wondered if he needed more. He decided to leave most of his supplies and equipment in the trailer, so he drove around the small pine trees and parked the overloaded trailer next to the big patio behind the house.

It took three days to clean and air out his new home, but on the third day, he moved his belongings into his new home. The cabin now had a strong pine and lemon scent that overpowered the musky smell. Joe could tolerate the new smell over the ones before that reminded him of death and despair.

He found a radio on a shelf in the living room and was able to get a few stations. Every day the news coming from the Far East sounded worst, and he felt the country might end up in a shooting war with North Korea and China over their constant cyber attacks on Taiwan and now the Philipines.

The last thing he did after getting all the dust and dirt cleaned was to take the sheets off the furniture only to find another note from his Grandma, which read:

Dear Joe:

I see you found the cabin and have probably cleaned it up a bit. It sure was dusty when I dropped by a year ago. Don't clean up the property much. It will be more difficult for people to find you and the cabin. Gramps and I became preppers when you were just a child, but your mom thought we were crazy, so we never talked about it; however, most of the games and treasure hunts you thought were fun were actually training. We used them to instill the need for secrecy and hopefully, you will remember where some of the hidden treasure is located if the shit hits the fan. I was open about my thoughts that an apocalypse was just around the corner, and I hope Gramps and I helped get you ready for it if and when it happens.

Love Grandma.

This message was a bit confusing because Joe only remembered bits and pieces of the early years up at the cabin. He did; however, remember learning how to hunt fish, clean game, and a million other tasks related to camping in the wild. Joe had an aha moment and realized that all of that was the training and treasure she talked about. Well, he didn't think there was going to be an apocalypse, but he could certainly use those skills to live off his land and avoid people. He would look for the treasure later.

The day after finding the main cabin, he took a break to explore the woods around the cabin and to look for the other two cabins that he remembered. They were on the map, so he used his GPS to help steer him toward the first. A further search revealed the second cabin was only a hundred yards from his new home. He was disappointed as he walked up to the cabin because he could see that the roof sagged and the door was hanging open. The cabin had not been kept up and had fallen apart. In ten years it would be one with the woods around it.

He continued east, walking through the tough, thick brush until he knew he was a few hundred feet south of the third cabin. Joe had to crawl part of the way up the mountain since it was too steep to walk but not vertical enough to climb. He was out of breath when he arrived at the cabin.

This structure was in good shape but was more rustic than his new home. It was more like what he had expected to find. It didn't have electricity, propane heat, or a pump to get running water into the very rustic cabin. There was an old well that had seen better days. He took the wad of keys he had found in the pouch, opened the door and looked around. The furniture was covered with sheets. Although the cabin was a beautiful little place to live he decided to stick with his more modern cabin. He took a different route back to his home.

After cleaning the entire house including the basement, he loaded the spoiled food into his trailer and headed back to town to dump the trash and purchase enough groceries to last him a couple of weeks. He remembered that Grandma had told him of the fierce winters and deep snow in the mountains. He also stopped by the bank and left with $10,000 cash which he converted to old silver coins and small silver bars on the recommendation of one of his survival books.

After he had finished his errands, he heard on the truck's radio that banks had closed before noon and that the entire financial system of the USA had been hacked. A voice on the radio said, "One of our financial experts says that the cyber attack destroyed all records in 80 percent of America's banks and that no one could tell how much money they had in their bank accounts and all mortgage info had been lost."

Another expert reported that all stock trading records had been wiped out in the USA, Japan, and Europe. Millions of people were flocking to their bank to get their money out. Joe quickly realized that his valuable stock was now worthless.

Joe doubled back to check with his bank. There he found a huge crowd gathering at each of the banks on the block. Police cars were pulling up as fights broke out in the crowd. Joe floored his Bronco, and a few minutes later, he heard the radio emergency broadcast warning. He pulled over to focus on the alert as he saw people streaming out on to the streets.

The announcer said to keep all radios and TVs tuned to the Conelrad Emergency Broadcast station during this dire emergency. He then introduced the President who said, "My fellow Americans, our country suffered a horrendous cyber attack on our financial system just a few hours ago, and now New York, Chicago, and Los Angeles have been attacked with small thermo-nuclear dirty bombs by Islamic terrorists. Though these bombs were small in yield, consisting of military grade explosives attached to the radioactive material, the damage is substantial. Our military is responding ... Oh, my God. Numerous missiles are inbound. Seek shelter..." The voices were replaced with static, and then the radio went silent.

He saw two cars collide ahead of him and heard crashing sounds behind him. Only an old pickup truck was moving, and every driver was getting out of their stalled vehicles. One of the vehicle's gas tank had ruptured, and gas flowed toward several other cars. The gas ran under a crashed car and erupted in flames. Soon several cars were on fire, and one exploded. The smoke from the burning tires was black and acrid as it burned Joe's lungs.

Several people were injured in the crashes, and good Samaritans were checking on them. The Bronco's engine was still running so he started to pull around several stalled cars when he heard a terrible roar above as a shadow blocked out the sun. A few seconds later, a Boeing 737 Airliner crashed into the side of Mount Ashland. The crash was followed by a huge rolling cloud of black smoke. Joe was certain no one had survived.

Joe didn't even have time to think before several other explosions came from the direction of the Medford airport. Planes were dropping out of the sky, and thousands of people were dying around him. One of the aircraft struck a factory, and there were multiple secondary explosions after the initial crash. He heard a deafening sound coming from his left and saw a small jet gliding down to the ground without power. Joe then noticed that Cobb's Outfitters and Outdoors Store was in the path of the plane. The plane struck the ground in the parking lot of Cobbs and slammed into the building. It exploded sending flames and smoke skyward. He thought about that raven-haired beauty in the camping supplies department and thought what a waste of a gorgeous woman. Damn.

Joe was frightened and headed out of town as quickly as the vehicle would go. Several minutes later he heard gunfire. He saw two older vehicles fleeing town and heading east on Dead Indian Road. One of them, a black Jeep, turned off on the same road that he took to get to the cabin. The Jeep kept going northeast when the road forked, and Joe took the eastern route to his cabin. He flew up the side roads and dirt paths back to the cabin.

Joe only knew something horrible was happening to his country. He didn't know much about the financial system or nuclear Electromagnetic Pulse bombs. He just knew the shit had hit the fan and it was the end of the world as we know it. He arrived at the cabin and turned the radio on to only hear static. He drank several bottles of beer down as he sat in the basement, collected his thoughts, and let his nerves calm down.

That's how Joe Harp left civilization and disappeared into the Oregon woods before the world's financial collapse, and nuclear EMP attacks caused civilization to fall apart. Billions of his fellow men would die over the next few months. Joe wasn't a prepper or a survivalist. He was an average Joe who made a living fixing cars, and now he was fighting to survive.

It was pure luck and a couple of good decisions that had helped Joe survive the first days of the world's collapse. Now he would need to learn quickly how to survive, or he would be just another casualty in the billions who died that year and would never be remembered.

Joe dropped to his knees, looked to heaven, and thanked God for delivering him. He realized that he was one of the luckiest men on earth to have received this myriad of blessings in such a timely manner. He thought, *Yeah, I'm lucky, but right now it looks like only the lucky will survive this debacle.*

Chapter 3

Constance May Simms was a divorced single mother who had sacrificed every day for ten long hard years so her daughter could have a good life and get an excellent education. She gave birth to Cloe when she was only 15 and had to drop out of school. Her jock boyfriend did marry her but quickly ditched her when she interfered with his college and womanizing. Cobie was 18, divorced, and uneducated when she entered the workforce. She was too proud to go back home to her mom and stepdad. She lived on welfare and WIC while working as much as she could until she was able to get Cloe into kindergarten and started her first job that paid above minimum wage.

Cobie got her nickname from her younger stepbrother when saying Cobie was the best he could do as he tried to say Connie's name. She was five foot four, weighed 115 pounds, and had jet black hair to go along with her outgoing disposition. She had hazel eyes and a smooth blemish free skin that made her look younger than her 29 years. While she was beautiful, it was in a Tomboy sort of fashion.

While a very outgoing and friendly person, Cobie rarely had time to date working two jobs and raising her twelve-year-old daughter. Every dime she earned went to make sure that Cloe had as good a life as possible even though Cobie had to sacrifice her social life and remain single. They had moved several times as Cobie found better jobs and could afford to move to towns with better schools for Cloe. They were living their dream in Ashland, Oregon when the bottom fell out due to the eviction from their apartment, which had been their home for the past three years.

While Cobie waited on the Sheriff, her mind drifted back to her heated discussion with the property manager and specifically to the handsome, though overweight, young man. Cobie had trouble keeping focused on the jerk who was evicting her and her daughter because there was just something special about the man. She wished she had gotten his name. He disappeared into the Archery department before Cobie could fake bumping into him. Her face was hot and flushed as she thought about the man. Even though she had avoided dating for years, this man was like a moth to a flame to her. She couldn't resist following him in the store and watching him until a customer needed her and she lost track of him.

The Sheriff and his men that would be tossing her out of the apartment showed up at 3:00 sharp. Cobie had already loaded the back seat of her Jeep with their clothes, camping gear, and bags of food from the kitchen. She made sure her guns and ammo were hidden under the clothes in the back seat. She had borrowed a small trailer from her boss at the store and had the men load the rest of her possessions on the trailer. Cobie had arranged for her daughter to stay with a friend overnight while she sorted out where they would live until she could find a place.

She had looked for two months to no avail because she couldn't afford any apartments or houses in Ashland. She tried renting a single room from several good-hearted people, but they wouldn't let Cloe's dog stay at their home. Cobie had promised her 12-year-old daughter that she wouldn't move again until Cloe graduated high school. Cobie and Cloe had been moving around since the divorce, and since Cobie had no skills, she couldn't find decent paying jobs. That meant they couldn't afford a suitable place to live. Ashland was a high-cost city, but Cloe loved the school, and all her friends went to school in Ashland.

Cobie sat in her Jeep for a minute to collect herself. She drove to a cheap hotel and would stay there until she figured out what to do. Several days later she was at work when a solution jumped out at her. She sat in her Jeep and wiped away the tears and steeled herself to the fact that they might have to move to a poor section of Medford when she saw the camping gear. A brainstorm hit her, and she backed out of the driveway heading to the mountains. The camping gear reminded her of a conversation she overheard between her boss and one of the customers. The customer complained that he hated leaving his cabin unattended most of the winter and that he wouldn't use it again until late spring. Her boss mentioned that most of the cabins around Ashland were left unattended for months and that they were rarely broken into so he shouldn't worry.

That's when Cobie decided to squat at someone's cabin until they could find a place of their own. They wouldn't damage anything, and if caught she would plead for forgiveness and move to another cabin. She parked the trailer behind the store and headed out to find a cabin.

Cobie wanted to remain close to her job and Cloe's school, so she found several old maps of the mountains around Ashland at the library. She made notes about trails and cabins in the area to shorten her search. Cobie drove up Dead Indian Road and turned off to the right after a few miles to search for several cabins that were on top of a ridge about three fourths up the side of the mountain.

The temperature dropped as she drove up the mountainside. The Jeep was warm on the inside, and she wasn't prepared for the temperature drop or the snow on the ground. The air was brisk and smelled of Pine; each breath made her question her brainstorm. *It was damned cold up here in the mountains*, she thought.

The first cabin's door was broken and only hanging by one hinge. All of the windows were broken, and beer bottles and cans were strewn around the outside of the cabin. Cobie drove deeper into the woods heading west and found two burned out cabins before the road ended. She looked at her copy of one of the maps and saw there should be two cabins below her location. One back in the direction she had come and another directly below her present position. The maps were old, but with luck, the cabin would still be there and usable.

Cobie put her hooded jacket on, stuck her .380 Ruger in her Santis pocket holster, and headed down the steep terrain to find the cabin. The brush was thick, and Cobie struggled to make her way down the hill without falling. The combination of the dense undergrowth and snow made the going treacherous; she slipped several times until she fell and rolled down the hill, hit something, and lay there with the wind knocked out of her aching body.

"Crap, that hurts," Cobie murmured as she rubbed her butt and checked herself for broken bones and other injuries.

She lay there flat on her butt for a minute with her eyes closed thinking how stupid this whole thing was when she opened her eyes and saw the wall of the cabin above her.

"Darn, it's a building. I'm in luck. It's the cabin I was looking for."

The cabin was covered with vines and had small trees and bushes growing up next to it making it virtually invisible from a distance. No one would come to this place and evict her. It looked as if no one had been here for many years. Cobie cautiously walked around the cabin and noted all of the windows were secured with shutters, and both of the cabin doors were intact and closed. She tried the front door, and the knob wouldn't turn. She walked around to the rear of the cabin and couldn't budge that doorknob either, so she tried moving one of the shutters that covered a window facing out over the back deck. She pulled on the shutter, and it fell apart in her hands and fell to the deck.

The window wouldn't move at first, but soon it rose a bit after Cobie pulled upward with all of her strength. The window was open, and she removed a flashlight from her coat pocket and looked inside the cabin. She stared into the kitchen and looked over the kitchen sink. There was no danger in sight, so she climbed into the room and stepped down to the floor from the counter. The kitchen was dusty and had a lot of cobwebs but otherwise was in great shape.

The dank, musty smell hit her, and she said," Holy crap that stinks like a burial vault."

The kitchen was right out of the late 1800's complete with an old cast iron cooking stove and one of those steel cupboards covered in white enamel with a red pinstripe. There was an old-fashioned hand pump by the side of the sink and an old wooden icebox in the corner. The kitchen table was solid oak with four ladder back chairs with cane bottoms.

Cobie explored the rest of the small cabin and found it had two bedrooms, a small family room, bathroom, and the kitchen. The larger bedroom had an old iron bed with a feather mattress, and both were covered in dust. The dresser was oak and had a large mirror. The mirror tilted so the lady of the house could sit in front of it and put her makeup on by the light of two small kerosene lamps. Cobie laughed when she thought about a woman sitting in front of this charming dresser putting makeup on in such a crappy cabin.

It was less than 900 square feet but would be perfect for their needs. Cobie made notes on what she needed to clean the cabin and then headed back to her Jeep to go fetch her trailer. She would work all night on the cabin to make it clean enough to bring Cloe to their new home. The only negative was she saw a few footprints in the dust but couldn't tell if they were new or years old.

The furniture was covered in sheets, and everything had a thick layer of dust. Cobie removed the sheets from the furniture and found a handwritten note. The note read:

Dear Joe:

So, you found this ratty old cabin while exploring your new property. This cabin was originally built in the 1850's when Oregon was settled. Your grandfather and I stayed in it for years until we built the other cabins. I hope you never have to live in this ragtag excuse of a cabin, but once it had a family that loved it and depended on it for their survival. Please don't tear it down because it holds many a memory and was the place where your dad was conceived. I know TMI.

Love Grandma.

Cobie almost cried because the old woman apparently loved her grandson and the old cabin. Then she wondered if Joe actually lived in the woods nearby.

She opened the windows and doors to let light in and air out the place as she dusted and then wet mopped the floors. The pump didn't work, but there was a small creek twenty yards from the west side of the cabin with ice cold, clear water. She found two buckets and hauled water into the bathtub and sink. She scrubbed the bathroom first and kept a bucket of water in the room to flush the toilet. Then she cleaned the two bedrooms and drug the mattresses outside to air out. It was 1:00 am when she finished the last room and fell asleep on the couch.

Cobie woke several times to the sound of a wolf howling in the early morning hours, and it sent shivers up her back as she snuggled deeper into her sleeping bag. She thanked God her boss had allowed her to purchase the slightly damaged camping gear at a reduced rate, now that she needed it to help make a home for her daughter. The sleeping bag was one of the best, and she had to strip down to her underwear during the night to keep from sweating. Unfortunately, she almost froze as she put her clothes back on the next morning and since she didn't build a fire, the toilet seat was like a block of ice. Perhaps camping in the winter was not her cup of tea but it beat living on the streets with her twelve-year-old daughter.

She made it to work on time and thanked her boss for allowing her to leave the trailer there while she apartment hunted. She evaded his questions about the location of her new digs and only said that it was a small home out in the country but still in the Ashland school district.

Cobie had the radio on while waiting on Cloe to get out of school and the station broke into another song to announce there was turmoil in Asia between China and Taiwan. Cobie never watched the national news and frankly didn't give a care about national or world events. She knew who the President was by name but didn't know the Oregon Congressmen. She had a daughter to raise, and anything else was just background noise, so she changed the channel only to hear the same crap coming out of the speaker.

She smiled when she saw her mini-me walking with a boy to the Jeep. Cloe was two inches shorter and fifteen pounds lighter but could pass for her mother though Cobie was 16 years older. They shared most of their clothes and even wore the same shoe size. Cloe looked much older for her age

40

and could pass for a twenty-year-old the same as her mom. Several people had stopped them while out shopping and thought they were twin sisters. This made Cloe happy and put a frown on Cobie's face because she wanted her little girl to grow up slower and more sheltered than she had.

The young man peeled away as Cloe arrived at the Jeep making her mom ask, "Who is your new friend and how old is he?"

"Mom, his name is Brad, and he is only a bit older than me. He's 16 and has a Mustang. We just talk and have a Trig class together."

Bennie, Cloe's chocolate colored Lab, jumped in Cloe's lap as Cobie said, "Cloe, you are twelve years old and are a freshman. You are brilliant but not mature. You are too young to go with a boy four years older with a car. Does he know you are only twelve?" a protective mother exclaimed.

"Mom, please. It's not like we're having sex or anything. He hasn't even tried to kiss me yet," Cloe said as she baited her mom.

"Cloe, I have a gun and can get a fingerprint kit. If he touches you, I will shoot him in his ..."

"Balls, mom, that's what they call them these days," replied Cloe as she laughed at her mom.

"Girl, we are going to our new home after we drop by the store to get some paint, hammer, and nails. I think you will like our new rustic home," Cobie crossed her fingers as the words came out of her mouth.

"Mom, what street is it on? Is it close to the school? Do any of my friends live nearby?"

Cobie answered, "Don't know, no, and probably not. It's a cabin in the woods and kind of off by its self. It's all we could afford, and it's about six miles out of town."

Cloe thought for a minute and then asked, "Which direction?"

Her mom pointed straight up, "It's kinda up in the hills east of here. I love it, and we can walk in the woods and commune with nature. Bennie will love it."

"If the wolves don't eat him first. Mom, I will love anywhere you choose for us to live. I hope you know that I know how much you do to make a good home for me."

She shook her finger at her daughter, "Buttering me up won't make me change my mind about that boy."

"Mom!"

Cobie drove to the ridge above the cabin and asked her daughter to help carry the supplies down the steep path to the cabin.

"Mom, where is the house and why isn't there a mailbox?"

"I'll explain everything once we make about three trips down to the cabin. The cabin is about 200 feet down the hill and hasn't been used in a long time. The going will be rough. Follow me and watch where you step," replied Cobie.

As Cobie warned, the going was tough, but they arrived at the cabin, and Cloe loved their new home, "Mom, this is great. The path is horrible, but I love the cabin and the woods. Bennie will love romping in the trees."

They made two more trips with Bennie running along with them barking and chasing a rabbit. Cobie made sure they entered the woods from a different place so they wouldn't wear a path in the foliage by the old road. She then had all of the trails converge about 25 feet down the hill so most of the way to the cabin could be cleared. Earlier she had walked around the woods and never found a path to the cabin. It was surrounded by dense stands of trees, brush, and weeds.

Cobie turned a portable kerosene heater on in the living room, the kitchen and living room were soon reasonably warm.

"Mom, we don't have central heating?"

"Darling, this is a hunter's cabin and wasn't meant to be lived in year round. We will live like the pioneers did 150 years ago with a wood burning fireplace and well water. I'm sorry but there just wasn't much in our price range in the school district. As a matter of fact, we will get our mail from Joan's house to make sure no one questions if you live in the Ashland school district," Cobie replied anxiously.

"I really like the cabin, and the walk down will only be twice a day, so I'll get used to it. Darn, do we have to heat water for our baths? Oh, crap, there is no shower," a shocked look came over the poor teenager's face.

Cobie tried to look sympathetic as she responded, "No darling, there is no shower, and yes we have to heat the water for a bath. I'll work on installing a shower a bit later, but you'll have to rough it for a while.

It was soon dark, and Cobie lit the kerosene lanterns and prepared supper while Cloe worked on her homework. They both were somewhat amazed at how quiet the cabin and surrounding woods were at night until they heard the first wolf howl after supper.

"Mom was that a wolf howling. How neat."

Cobie had her .380 gripped tightly and was shivering at the sound of the animals as one after another answered the call of the wild. She was having second thoughts about living in the woods as Cloe and she got into bed that night.

"Mom supper was great, and I've finished my homework, so is it okay if I watch some TV?"

"Oops, Cloe, remember my comments about living like pioneers. Well, pioneers didn't have TVs. Don't worry. I'll rig up my cell phone as a hotspot, and we can watch TV through the internet until we figure out how to have a real TV."

"Mom, we've been studying solar cells in science class. We could get some solar cells and a battery-powered TV. We'll need solar cells to charge our cell phones anyway."

Cobie turned the radio on, and to her dismay every one of the stations had the president talking about a crisis with China. She turned it off, but Cloe turned it back on and said, "Mom that sounds serious. I think we need to pay attention because the president said we could soon be at war with China. War with China could mean nukes, and nukes mean the world could get all ... err ... fouled up."

The president's speech only lasted half an hour, and then Cloe found a station with pop music and they listened to it as they played scrabble the rest of the night until bedtime. Cobie gave Cloe the bedroom that she had cleaned and slept on the couch with both of them bundled up in their own sleeping bags to ward off the cold. The kerosene heater would heat up the entire cabin, but Cobie was afraid they would die from carbon monoxide poisoning as they slept.

Cobie woke up before dawn and lit the heater so the cabin would be warm for Cloe's bath. Then she started a fire in the wood-burning kitchen stove to heat water for their baths. The stove boiled the water and warmed the kitchen quickly, so she woke her daughter and told her to bathe before the water got cold. Cloe stripped down, jumped in the tub, and suddenly realized the room wasn't as warm as she was used to when she got out of the tub.

"Mom, I'm freezing it's frigging cold in here."

"Watch your mouth young lady, but you are correct. I think we need to move bath time to just before bed, so we don't freeze. The cabin will be nice and warm then," she laughed as she dreaded the cold room.

They drove into town that morning, and Cobie dropped her daughter off at school and headed to work. The sales had doubled this week due to the ongoing threat of war. All of the preppers were buying supplies, solar cells, water purification tablets, aluminum bags for Faraday Cage protection for electronics from EMP radiation, and emergency food rations. Cobie hid one of the lower priced solar cell kits and one of the Faraday bags. She called her friend Joan and had her purchase them for her. Cobie also purchased some water purification tablets and made a mental note to buy some unscented bleach on the way home. She would treat the water from the creek until they could get the well working.

Cobie had a long line of customers in the camping department when the store manager made an announcement over the PA, "The store is closing in five minutes. The president has just announced that we are at war with North Korea, Iran, and China and could face immediate nuclear attack. Store employes, please stay at your stations until all customers have left the store."

Cobie grabbed her solar cell kit, a couple of walkie-talkies and batteries, and an emergency radio. She then took a bag full of MREs and grabbed a half dozen boxes of .22 LR for Cloe's pistol as she ran out the back door of Cobb's Outfitters on her way to her Jeep. She placed the electronics in the aluminum bag and drove off the lot. She raced through the streets and around traffic jams by driving through people's yards and down sidewalks.

She arrived at Cloe's school and walked to the front door, which was locked. She pounded on the door until the Vice-Principle came to the door.

"Lady, we are on lockdown until the crisis is over. Your kid will be safer here than at home."

Cobie drew her .380 shot a bullet through the glass beside the man. The glass exploded into the building, and the sound frightened the man.

Cobie said, "You will die here and now if you don't bring my daughter to me now."

The Vice-Principle screamed, "Jim, get Cloe Simms. Now!"

A minute later Cloe came running to the door and left with her mother as the Vice-Principle yelled, "I'm calling the police. You will go to jail!"

Cloe looked at her mom and saw rage and fear on her face and asked, "Mom, what's wrong? You scared the crap out of Mr. Jenkins."

"I'll explain in a few minutes. We have to head for the cabin now. The country is under attack," Cobie's face was red and was focused on saving her daughter's life.

Cloe turned the radio on and heard the Emergency Broadcast System blaring out warnings. Then abruptly only static could be heard, and then the radio stopped making any sound at all. Several cars stalled ahead of them, and then a truck barreled through the intersection ahead and t-boned a minivan full of people. The streets erupted into chaos with injured people falling out of their wrecked cars and others looking at their dead iPhones. There was an explosion a few miles away. Suddenly there was a roar, and a jet slammed into the school they had just left, and another jet hammered into Cobb's Outfitters.

Cloe hit her dazed mom on the shoulder and said, "Mom our Jeep is still running, let's go home now before this gets ugly."

Cobie shook her head, floored the gas peddle, and popped the clutch squealing tires as she flew around the stalled cars. She cut through the median and ran through a chain link fence to get on Dead Indian Road on her way to the cabin. She saw two more vehicles heading out of town and noticed one was an old Ford pickup and the one behind her was an old Bronco. She didn't make the connection then but thanked her father several times later for buying the old Jeep for her.

They were soon on the ridge overlooking the hill where their cabin was located. Cobie parked the Jeep and started to get out when Cloe said, "Mom, we have to hide the Jeep. All of the new cars died when the planes crashed. There was a solar flare or an EMP blast nearby. We studied them last year, and since we are at war with China, my bet is an EMP. Everyone will try to steal our Jeep."

"Great idea," Cobie replied as she picked a spot to drive the jeep into the woods and down the hill a bit to a flat place to leave the vehicle out of sight from the old road.

"Grab that bag while I carry the rest of my stuff. We need to hunker down and hide until we know what dangers lurk out in the world. Baby girl, I watched that Doomsday show on TV last year, and the world could get real mean if we have lost all power and the food in stores run out. There will be riots and people killing each other so they can feed their families."

They walked down the hillside to the cabin, and Bennie greeted them on the back deck. Cloe ran inside and turned the radio on to catch any news on the crashed airplanes and find out if there were any survivors at the school and store. The radio didn't come on at all, so Cloe checked her phone, and it was dead.

"Mom, my phone is dead, check yours,"

Cobie pulled her phone from her back pocket, and the screen was dark and would not power up, "I think those people at the store were right; we've been nuked. Hey, grab that shiny bag by the front door and bring it to me in the kitchen."

Cloe took the emergency radio out of the bag and set it on the table while Cloe read the directions. Cobie turned it on, and nothing happened until Cloe started turning the hand crank and they heard static. Cloe turned the tuner knob to the frequency marked E-Broadcast and heard someone talking.

"... stay in your houses for at least three days until the debris, and radioactive particles have settled to the ground. Do not eat anything that has been exposed to the fallout. The president has called out the military and National Guard to ..."

The radio went silent, so they changed the channel until they heard a man talking on an AM channel.

" ... no atomic bombs in this area. An EMP blast above Central California has fried all electronics. I'm a prepper, so all of my equipment was in a Faraday cage. I'll broadcast every evening at about 7 pm starting today. I will pass on any news and give you some survival tips. This is VWPACKRAT signing off. Have a Happy Apocalypse."

"Mom WTF was that?"

"Apocalypse or not I will tan your butt for cursing," said Cobie.

"Mom, I'm sorry, but I spelled W...T...F and didn't say ... well, you know."

"I'll give you a pass today since that was a WTH moment."

"WTH?"

"What the heck. I still have to be a mom even in an apocalypse. I need you to fix supper while I check our other survival gear out."

She placed the batteries in the walkie-talkies and turned both on after reading the instructions. Their range was only 5-10 miles depending on the line of sight. She sent Cloe

49

outside with one, and they said hi to each other to make sure the radios worked. While Cloe finished preparing soup and sandwiches, Cobie tried all of the channels and heard a man crying as he asked someone for help to get his wife to the hospital. A different channel had a truck driver who was pinned in his truck after it crashed down a mountainside.

☆

Chapter 4

His sleep was interrupted several times by nightmares about him catching Gwen and Darren in the Explorer and then shooting them. The other dreams centered on bears and mountain lions eating him as he struggled to survive. He woke up between nightmares to go to the bathroom several times because the beer was working overtime on his bladder. Lack of sleep and the nightmares caused him to be half-asleep and scared as he sat down at the kitchen table to eat breakfast, which consisted of cereal, milk made from powder and water, Coke, and a Rogue River IPA.

He played with the last floating fruity chunks of cereal in his bowl while thinking about what the hell he had to do today. He didn't think about the horrible events that occurred the previous day and was still working on his original plan to live alone in the woods. He was one lucky man that the plan he should have been working on had many of the same items as his original plan. Joe was in denial and would be in a fog for several weeks. He only thought about staying away from people and living his life on his own terms on his piece of land in the woods of Oregon.

He looked over at the table and saw the book of letters from his Grandma and remembered to read the remaining three messages that she had told him to read first. The note read:

Dear Joe:

You need to take an inventory of all of the supplies and food and see what needs to be replaced. You need to keep three to six months worth of food stored at all times in case you get snowed in, or TEOTWAWKI happens. Those damn Russians, Iranians, and Koreans will eventually attack the USA. Be prepared for anything.

Love Grandma.

Joe spent the next day opening all of the boxes in the basement and carefully recording the contents on a list. He found several cases of seeds and other supplies to help him start a large garden. He also found several cases of pool shock with notes on how much to add to water to purify it to kill all germs. Many of the boxes contained board games and fiction and nonfiction books. His favorite finds were boxes containing all the supplies one needed to make ale and distill whiskey. He still avoided thinking about the disaster that was unfolding around him and tried to focus on the cabin and its contents.

The next morning Joe started his work by putting away the supplies he had purchased in town the other day. After a dozen trips up and down the basement stairs, he had moved everything from the trailer to the basement. He now had a two-week supply of food and another week or two of the survival food that was still fit to eat. On one of his trips to the basement, he brought up a stack of books on trapping, survival, and living off the grid.

He opened a large metal locker and found several walkie-talkies, a CB radio, and a Ham radio set up. There were batteries and a fold-up solar cell power generator. The cabinet also contained several manuals and books on the devices. He took them upstairs, placed them on the kitchen counter, and went on about his business.

On several occasions, he thought he heard something in the woods and felt someone was watching him as he worked to carry the supplies into the house. He even saw a dog chasing a rabbit and wondered about the millions of dogs that wouldn't be fed by their owners as they struggled to feed themselves. This reminded him to strap his .44 Magnum on his hip and always be prepared to defend himself.

The next chore was to fill the cistern with water from the well out back of the cabin. The house initially had solar-powered lights and a water pump that sent water from the well into the large cistern on the back of the cabin. Joe couldn't get it working and thought the batteries were shot. He had purchased a voltmeter and had placed fixing the solar powered system on his To Do list. Until then he had to power the pump at the well from his Bronco's battery. An hour and a half later, the cistern was filled. Joe learned quickly to turn the motor off and on to keep the battery charged while still conserving gasoline.

The sun was no longer directly overhead, and Joe was hungry, so he went into his new home and prepared a peanut butter sandwich and the milk left over from this morning. He hadn't built a fire yet, so the cabin was about the same temperature as the outside, which was 34 degrees according to the thermometer on the back patio. He added an apple to his meal and reminded himself that he could cook a real dinner that night. He saw the books in front of him and thumbed through several before deciding to go on a hike and blow off work the rest of the day.

He slung his backpack over his shoulders and hooked the clasps before picking up his .308 Savage and his map. He made up his mind to explore a small section of his land every day until he had covered every square foot of the area. Joe looked at his map and knew the lines gave him an idea of the elevation and quickly figured out that his land was almost square, had a valley running through the center and rose 200 feet on the north end and only 50 on the south side. He thought about it for a few minutes and decided it was like an inverted saddle with the cabin on a flat spot about halfway up the northern hills. He headed north directly behind the cabin and found the going very tough. The land was primarily on the top of a mountain range and was rocky with a lot of scrub brush and trees.

Joe had to climb steep hills several times until he was at the top of the ridge behind the cabin and the map indicated he was now on Forest Service property. There was an old service road on top of the hill, and he found more fresh tire tracks in the snow heading east. From this height, Joe could look a hundred feet over the cabin back toward Ashland. The cabin wasn't visible, but he knew he would have to make sure he only burned firewood at night, or someone on top of the hill could see the smoke. This was the minute that Joe realized that he was alone and the world had changed forever.

Joe walked for over an hour on top of the ridge to make sure no one lived in the area and found nothing. He then walked on top of the ridge heading west until he thought he was on the corner of his property and headed down the snow-covered and very slippery hill to see what was in that area. He found the going very tough and had to make his way sideways several times before he could head down the rocky hill again. Joe found himself hugging a large rock outcropping with his feet slipping on the snow to make it down the hill. He saw something to his left when the ledge he was on widened out enough to turn around. It was a cave.

Joe pulled his flashlight out of his pack and drew his revolver before walking into the opening. The opening was only four feet high, so he kept the flashlight, and his pistol pointed ahead of him as he slowly advanced into the darkness. There was a foul odor springing from the cave. Joe stopped and tied his handkerchief over his nose so he could proceed. After ten feet the ceiling sloped upward, and just as he could stand up, Joe saw the first bear and then saw several others. It was still winter, and he had walked into a den of hibernating bears. He slowly backed out of the cave and made a beeline straight down the hill. He made two mental notes. The first was to stay away from sleeping bears. The second was the location of an abundant food source if things ever get rough, he could kill and eat the bears.

He walked west until he saw water cascading down the rocks into a pool below, which fed a small creek that wound its way down the hillside. He walked along the creek bank until he arrived at a pool where the hillside ended, and the level spot allowed the water to pool then fall over a rock ledge to flow on down to the valley below. He was deep in thought about this being a great spot to swim when the water warmed. He was brought out of his daydream when he saw several human footprints mixed in with a dog's prints. The human prints were too small for a man, and he thought they had to be a woman's or a child's footprints. He knew they weren't very old but didn't know enough about tracking to see they were only a day old.

Joe knew that people hiked in the public forests and perhaps someone had strayed down the hill following the stream. He walked on down to the other side of the valley through a large meadow and then walked back west in the tree line so he wouldn't be seen if there were people around. He got closer to the path to the cabin and walked further east until he turned north. Then he climbed up a slope to a vantage point where he pulled out his binoculars and gazed at the city of Ashland below.

Even after three days, the fires started by the plane crashes still threw off thick black smoke. Joe was shocked to see fires raging at several large buildings that he thought had been located at the Mall of Ashland. He also saw a massive fire that he thought was at the University of Southern Oregon. Joe saw these things and felt sorry for those people, but it didn't register with him that this was the end of the world. He scanned the skyline and saw billowing clouds of smoke above

Medford and then packed his binoculars and headed back to the safety of his cabin.

The sun was setting in the west, and it was already dark and much colder in the woods around the cabin. He walked up the steps, looked for any trace of visitors, and saw none. He decided then to bring sand from the nearby creek and spread it on the deck and patio so he could see if anyone had been snooping around. He made it a habit from then on to smooth out the sand before entering or leaving the cabin.

Joe started a fire in the fireplace for the first time since he had been at the cabin. The warmth of the fire made him feel good as he read several of the survival books that evening. He loved the smell of the wood smoke but knew the cancer rates in the new world would skyrocket. Before turning in for the night, he added several more logs to the hearth and checked to make sure the fire screen was in place.

He woke up the next morning to a chill in the air and hated to get out of his sleeping bag. He didn't want to use the propane for heat and would keep it solely for cooking. He quickly changed his hygiene habits to fit his new lifestyle and decided he would only bathe every third day. He could stand the odor, and it wasn't like there were any hot chicks around to impress. He applied his deodorant before dressing and said aloud, "Holy crap. Where will I get deodorant?"

No one answered, and then he said, "It's okay to talk out loud. What's not okay is answering yourself. Then again, who can better understand my problems, than me?"

Joe opened a can of Spam, sliced off two thick slabs, and placed them between two crackers for breakfast. He walked outside still munching on one of his Spam sandwiches when he saw dog tracks in the sand on the front porch. Before he had time to think a chocolate colored Lab ran onto the deck and begged for a bit of Joe's breakfast. He tore off a small piece, and the dog took it from his hand and quickly swallowed the meat and cracker. Joe wondered if the dog was the same one whose tracks were at the creek on the east side of his property. He checked the dog's collar, and it had Bennie and a phone number to call if the dog was lost.

Joe played with Bennie for a while and gave him half a can of Spam. The dog was hungry and gobbled the food down in seconds then unexpectedly left running into the woods. Joe was all alone, and the dog had been good company.

***

"Mom, Bennie disappeared this morning. I'm going to call for him to come home."

Cobie was deep in thought when she heard her daughter yell, "Bennie."

Cobie ran outside and admonished Cloe for yelling, "Baby, someone could hear you and come searching for us. Please don't do that again. Bennie will come back when he's through chasing rabbits. I hope he catches one, so we don't have to keep feeding him."

"Mom, we can't let him starve."

Cobie steeled herself and said, "Baby, we have to survive ourselves, or there won't be anyone to take care of

Bennie. If you stop feeding him, he will find game and eat like dogs have eaten for millions of years."

***

The dog's ears perked up, and he ran off into the woods at the same time Joe thought he heard a faint voice coming through the woods. He waited for a few minutes with his ear cocked toward the woods to the east but didn't hear anything, so he went back into the cabin and made a list of tasks to perform and another list of things to fetch from town.

Joe looked at his task list and saw he needed a bunch of car batteries for his solar energy generator's storage. He didn't want to run into town but remembered there were stalled cars that would never run again. He saw hundreds of stalled cars in Ashland but didn't want to risk going into town, but he knew there was a small strip mall close to where Dead Indian Road dead-ended into Highway 66 on the east side of Ashland.

Joe strapped on his .44 Magnum, placed a Glock 17 - 9 mm pistol in his coat pocket, and set his 12 Gauge shotgun behind the driver's seat. He then retrieved a tool bag from the basement that had the tools he needed to get the batteries. He placed it in the Bronco before heading into town.

There wasn't anyone on the road, and it only took a few minutes for Joe to arrive a block from the strip mall. He parked the Bronco behind a car wash bay beside a large truck and used his binoculars to look for any dangers. He didn't see any people so he used a siphon hose to fill his jerry can twice. He dumped the first can into the Bronco to top it off and then placed the full can back on its rack.

The stores had been looted and all of their windows broken; a few were burned. Joe was pleased to see that except for a few with broken windows, the cars and pickups were intact. He went back to the car wash and drove on to the strip mall's parking lot. He didn't want to stay any longer than necessary, so he cut the battery cables and hold down clamps and quickly removed eight batteries from late model cars. He placed the batteries in the back of the Bronco and sped back up Dead Indian road thinking he had escaped anyone's notice.

***

Joe didn't see the men watching from the hillside and didn't waste any time getting back to the cabin. He would have been frightened if he had heard the men's conversation.

"Mathem, an older Bronco drove up to the mall below us and took several batteries from cars."

"Did you capture the Bronco?"

"No, he moved too fast, and we couldn't sneak up on him before he left. The good news is that Said didn't see him come or go, so that means he is held up a few miles from town up in those hills."

"Good news. Thanks, and keep an eye out for him. We need more vehicles if we want to ever get out of here and head back to Portland. Make sure you catch him on the next trip by placing a couple of men up that side road. They can block the road after he goes into town, and then they can shoot the bastard as he goes back to his hideout. Just don't damage the Bronco. Allahu Akbar."

***

Joe spent the rest of the day installing the batteries, but it was too late for them to charge because the sun was down below the tree line. He looked up and said, "Crap, there will only be about three hours of sunshine on the solar cells now and maybe six during the summer. I'll bet the trees have grown a bunch since Grandpa added the solar cells."

No one answered, so he nosed the Bronco into the bank of batteries, hooked up his jumper cables, and ran the engine to give the batteries a good charge. As the truck charged the batteries, he thought he would look around the cabin for another gas can so he could bring back extra fuel. Then he could keep the batteries charged until the sun shined on them longer as spring approached. He also pondered the wisdom of topping off a few of the trees before next winter to gain more charging time from the solar cells.

***

Cobie and Cloe took turns listening to the walkie-talkie and radio to get news about the apocalypse. Cobie wanted to know if there were many people nearby. They heard several families on the walkie-talkie who were very careful not to give their location. Cobie felt they were no danger to Cloe and herself. Then a bit later that day Cloe ran down to the stream where Cobie was trying to catch fish and said, "Mom listen to this conversation."

Cobie listened and was very upset as she heard the men's plan to stop a Bronco, shoot the owner, and steal his truck. What really scared her was that they mentioned the Bronco went up the same road that would take them to the ridge above their cabin.

"Thanks for manning the radio and don't worry too much about the conversation because those men are miles from here," Cobie told her daughter.

"But Mom, they mentioned Dead Indian Road and the second turn to the right. We live off that road. If those guys come looking for Bronco man they could find us. We need to hide the Jeep better," the young girl, pleaded.

☆

Chapter 5

Joe turned the radio on at 6:50 pm and waited for VWPACRAT to broadcast and was rewarded at 7:11 with, "This is the VWPACKRAT coming from beautiful downtown none of your damned business. If you are the bad guys, don't even think I will give any information concerning my whereabouts. I have friends I stay in touch with over my ham radio and will pass on what they know about their areas. First from JW in Tacoma. He reports most of the city has been burned and most of the people left town when the food ran out. Now all he sees is one gang trying to kill another.

BS In Eugene reports the city has finally been locked down by the good guys and there was a purge of gang members, skinheads, and other undesirables. They lost 90 percent of their people so far from murders and people fleeing into the countryside to try their hand at living off the land. There is peace, but they are praying they can survive until crops can be harvested.

"KW in Medford reports that the prison inmates have taken over the city and executed the mayor and all policemen. The convicts have reached out to the jailbirds in Ashland, but the Ashland asshats don't want to play nice with the criminals in Medford and want to keep the city to themselves.

Folks, I can't say enough that you shouldn't go into the cities because they are a cesspool of gangs fighting gangs. The Blacks are fighting the Whites, and the Latinos are fighting everyone. Hunker down and stay in your spider holes until these thugs kill each other off. Now I'll cover how to catch, clean, and cook Opossum."

Joe sat there at the kitchen table with tears welling in his eyes as soon as VWPACKRAT mentioned the conditions in Eugene because he knew his Aunt was probably dead by now. He had tried to keep his mind off his family and felt apprehension because he didn't know what was happening back in Murfreesboro with his parents. Joe knew his dad could take care of himself in the woods but they lived in a large suburb of Nashville and the situation there was probably just as bad as these other places. He resigned himself to never seeing his parents or friends in Murfreesboro ever again.

These thoughts made him very angry and feel very vulnerable out in the woods alone. He started making plans to better camouflage and improve his defenses. He fetched several survival manuals containing booby traps and defensive measures, and a copy of the US Army Improvised Munitions Handbook. He thumbed through them and wasn't pleased with what he saw on how to install defensive measures, booby traps, and killing the enemy before they killed you. He kept searching and found a prepper's book that had large snare traps, trip wires for killing or giving warning of intruders, and deadfalls. He made notes and then went to sleep.

All though it wasn't the new week yet he needed to hear from his Grandma, so he opened the first weekly letter even though he had more than two dozen of the others to still read. The letter read:

Dear Joe:

I hope this message finds you again at the cabin and in good health. I know your woman isn't with you because this letter is actually the last one written. I rewrote it a day after I heard about her whoring around with your buddy. They didn't deserve to die that way, but Karma can be a bitch.

Joe this might sound mean, but that woman was a conniving social climbing bitch, and I'm glad she is out of your life. You deserve better.

You won't find a new love here in the woods so venture out every now and then to the cities to meet a few people. Living alone might be desirable now but trust me living without a loved one in your life is a lonely existence.

Buy more food, guns, and ammunition

Love Grandma.

Joe thought he should have read half of these letters the day he got them and he would be much better prepared.

The next morning he finished a can of Spam and read several of the daily letters so he wouldn't forget them. He was three letters ahead of schedule and read:

Dear Joe:

I know you very well, and you are probably a week ahead on reading these letters. I'm not there to keep you from peeking ahead, but please read them as I asked. I think you still need me in your life and I also think I can teach you a thing or two from the grave.

Love Grandma.

Joe answered, "But Grandma, I miss you and like to hear from you. I'm alone out here, and I don't like alone as much as I thought I would."

Joe's mind heard, *"Suck it up buttercup."*

Joe finished breakfast and took inventory of his supplies and searched for items he could use to install his security system. He started off placing rattle cans around the perimeter of the cabin to warn him of anyone's approach. The cans hung from paracord that had been tied from tree to tree, and the cans contained a few pebbles that would rattle when the line was tripped. He also placed several cans on the paracord that were like bells with large bolts and nuts hanging down like clappers in a bell. Joe then constructed a dozen large snares using large saplings bent in half with paracord nooses staked out on the ground with a peg in a notch that kept the sapling from springing upward until the peg was disturbed. The trap wouldn't kill anyone but would yank their feet out from under them and might break their ankles. They might also catch some medium size game.

Joe then found several wide planks and cut them down to three-foot lengths and drove sharpened nails through them. He would place these inside every doorway and below every window to alert him of anyone breaking into the cabin. They would cause great pain to the jerks trying to rob or cause harm to him. Joe didn't use most of the best traps because they would also kill innocent people who were just trying to survive.

***

"Mom, that VWPACKRAT must be close to us because I have plotted every city he has mentioned reports from and we are in the center of the cities and towns," Cloe beamed at her brilliant deduction.

"I hate to burst your bubble, but the man could be anywhere since Ham radios can reach out many miles during the night with certain conditions. He could be in Boise reporting on the areas from where he receives reports. There are very few people east of Boise and fewer now. I'm not sure about Opossum, but we do need to set some traps and catch some rabbits and perhaps shoot a deer to add to our food supply," replied her mom.

"I won't ever eat a dirty old Opossum. They are nasty looking and greasy," stated a girl who had never been hungry a day in her life.

"You'll eat a dead Opossum found on the road three days old if you get hungry enough. Hey, that reminds me, have you been feeding Bennie?"

"No Mom, I think he has found another food supply. Look at his belly;" Cloe said as she rubbed Bennie's stomach, and then added, "He is so full he just wants to sleep."

Cobie walked over to Bennie and rubbed his stomach then looked around his muzzle and said, "He's been hunting. He has dried blood on his muzzle. We need to teach him to share."

Cloe changed the subject and said, "Mom, those men talking on the radio scare me. What can we do to keep them from finding us?"

"Baby girl, we can't use the fireplace in the daytime or shoot at game. We will have to dress warmly and hunt with traps and fish a lot. I think we may have to take turns at guard duty every night until we feel safer."

"How would that work? Would I get a gun?"

"Yes, we need to give you some more training on using a gun to defend yourself. I gave you gun safety training last year, and I know you know how to shoot but killing in self-defense is another matter. I'm not sure I could kill someone attacking me, but I know I would have no issue with shooting someone who attacked my baby girl."

Cobie took the Ruger 10/22 and Ruger MKIV pistol from the bedroom closet and gave Cloe a refresher course on gun safety, cleaning, and maintenance of guns. Then she gave her training on the art of killing animals including two-legged thugs. She used a laser bore sight to help her daughter practice dry firing with a spent shell in each gun. She was afraid to fire the weapons for fear of attracting unwanted attention.

Cobie looked at her daughter cleaning the pistol and said, "Cloe in a couple of days we'll take a hike on up the road into the mountains about three or four miles and kill some rabbits or perhaps a deer. We will hightail it back here before anyone can get a fix on our position."

"I'd like that. I'd hate to get in a gunfight and never have shot at a living thing."

☆

Chapter 6

Early in the morning, several days after TSHTF Cobie tried the radio and could faintly hear someone talking but couldn't understand what was being said. She tried the walkie-talkie and listened to a man tell a friend to not go near the grocery stores because there were looting and rioting. He said people were shooting each other as food ran out. Another channel had a woman asking anyone who heard her to please meet at the Ashland Catholic Church and bring food for the needy. She continued to listen to the voices as she packed

Cloe's and her backpacks with food, a small hiker's tent, and extra ammunition.

"Mom, we have some extra food."

"No, we don't. We have enough to last a month if we stretch it out. Baby, that could be someone trying to steal food from people who prepared for this crisis. Get dressed, we are going hunting. I want to be three miles east of here before the sun rises," Cobie pinched her daughter to motivate movement.

"I'm dressing as fast as I can at 3 am in the morning. Mom, are we going to have breakfast?"

"No, we will eat these Clif Bars when we get to our destination. Fill your water bottle after you get dressed. The snow is gone on the ridge, and we can travel without leaving tracks if we are careful," an impatient mother told her daughter.

Cobie wanted to spend two days out hunting about three miles east of the cabin. Since they couldn't leave Bennie locked up that long but couldn't have him barking Cobie made a muzzle out of shoestrings and strips from an old bed sheet.

Her daughter met Cobie outside after putting the homemade muzzle on Bennie in the house, and the dog immediately began rubbing the muzzle with its paws and rubbing its snout against a tree. Cloe hugged Bennie and tried to make him feel good about the muzzle without much success.

"Cloe, thread your belt through this pistol holster and sling the rifle over your shoulder. Both are on safe and leave them on safe unless I tell you to shoot or we are attacked and then use your judgment. Always shoot to kill if you have to shoot someone, and as I've been preaching, shoot them several times until you know they are dead. Your .22s don't pack much punch, but three or four of them will kill a man."

Cobie instructed, "Put your LED headlamp on red and let's head out. Stay two steps behind me and try not to break any limbs or step on anything that will make noise. When we get closer to the ridge, we'll turn off our lights and walk with the aid of the half moon."

Cloe followed her mom who had Bennie on a leash and ambled until they covered the distance to the ridge. Cobie picked up the pace heading east after attaining the top of the hill. Cloe slowed a bit when they entered the tree line. They had walked for about half a mile when Cobie smelled smoke and gave the clenched fist sign for Cloe to stop.

"I smell smoke and can't tell what direction it's coming from. We will continue east but please don't make any noise as we move on to our hunting ground," Cobie said in a hushed voice.

They walked through the woods and crossed several dry streambeds plus one creek that was 15 feet wide and deep in spots. Cobie headed south along the creek until she found several logs jammed into a pile and walked across on top of them. They walked on for another mile until they headed back up a steep hill peppered with pine trees. The pine needles were slick, and Cloe slipped once and slid fifty feet back down the hill.

"Mom, I'm falling!"

"Hush, be quiet!"

Cobie slid down the hill to check on her daughter and found her to be okay, so they started back up the hill.

"Mom, when it's safe around here I want to come back and slide down this hill, it was fun."

"Girl, you ain't right in the head. Now hush and follow me," Cobie warned her playful daughter.

The moon was overhead, and Cobie caught the reflection of the moon off something ahead. She steered toward the light and found a large pond on top of the hill that was spring fed from higher up the mountain. She made a mental note to come back and try their luck fishing. They walked around the edge of the water and saw a Buck and two Does watering.

In a hushed voice, Cloe urged her mom to shoot the deer, but the reply was, "No, we are too close to our cabin. We need to travel about another mile."

"Mom, how do you know how far we've traveled?"

"I'm counting the steps we take. I figure three miles should be about 6,000 of my short steps," she whispered back to her daughter.

"Mom, how are you keeping count with me falling and asking so many questions?"

"Easy, I ignore you and tie a knot in my string for every 100 paces. Now shut up before I lose count again. We'll be halfway to Kentucky if you don't stop pestering me," Cobie joked.

An hour later Cobie stopped to rest and eat their Clif bars. She untied Bennie's muzzle guard and fed him some leftover potted ham. He turned his nose up at first then wolfed it down when Cobie acted as if she was going to place the muzzle back on his snout.

"Bennie, I can't say I blame you for turning your nose up because I can't stand the stuff myself. Cloe, we are in our hunting area and can start looking for game to hunt," Cobie waved at her daughter.

"Mom, what can I kill with the .22 rifle?"

"Any small game such as rabbits, squirrels, opossum, and raccoons," her mom smiled.

The young girl's face screwed up, "I know you are kidding about raccoons and opossums, but I guess I can kill rabbits and squirrels to eat."

"You aren't hungry yet, or you wouldn't say that nonsense. I'll be hunting for larger game such as deer, bear, elk, and whatever big game is out here. Meat is meat from now on. Baby girl we only have a few weeks of food and need to stretch that out until we can grow crops and find farm animals to raise. Now let's hunt."

"Mom, how will you kill a bear with a shotgun?"

"Baby, I have a three-inch magnum slug shell in my shotgun. People use them for deer hunting," Cobie answered.

They tried to be quiet but made too much noise, which resulted in most game running or hiding as they approached. After two hours the sun rose above the eastern mountains, Cloe pointed northwest and said, "Well, at least someone is having breakfast. See the smoke."

Cobie searched the skyline and replied, "That is about two miles back and a mile above our place. If we ever shoot, I want to gather our game and head south about a mile before making camp and then hunt south of the camp."

They sat at the base of a large pine tree when Cloe saw a large rabbit just twenty feet away. She leveled her rifle, aimed, and dropped the rabbit in its tracks. She and her mom ran over to the rabbit, placed it in a pillowcase, and high fived to celebrate Cloe's success. Cloe shot another rabbit five minutes later and waved it in the air for her mom to see. They stopped and listened for a few minutes to see if anyone was nearby, and then they headed south for 2,000 paces and begun to look for a campsite along a dry stream bed. They were lucky to find a place where the stream cut deep into a hillside leaving an undercut that made a shallow cave in the rocky embankment.

"This is on a hill sloping down for several hundred feet above us and below. It's going to be hard to sleep without rolling down the hill. Why camp here," Cloe asked.

Cobie answered, "Baby girl, I don't have all of the answers on how to survive but this place has snow to keep the rabbit from spoiling and anyone coming up or down the hillside will make a lot of noise that will alert us to their presence. That's why I chose this spot. Please feel free to give me your opinions because I'm just doing the best I know how."

"Those are good reasons. I didn't mean to hurt your feelings, Mom. You are doing great."

The snow was deep against the bank a few yards from the spot they selected as a campsite and Cobie sent Cloe to fetch several pillowcases full of the snow back to the campsite as she cleaned the rabbit. She had Cloe fed the organs to Bennie who ate them with zeal even though it was all Cloe could do to keep from losing her breakfast.

Cobie placed the rabbit in a plastic bag and stuck it in a hole Cloe had dug into the bank and covered it with the snow.

They then covered the snow with large slabs of rock to keep animals from digging up their supper.

"This "natures" icebox would work for perhaps another month before we have to find other ways to keep meat from spoiling. I know that smoked dried meat will last for months and will be good to put in soups or eat like jerky, but I don't have a clue how to can meat and besides we don't have the equipment," Cobie told her daughter.

"Mom, look, there is a raccoon across from the creek bottom."

"Don't shoot near our camp. We don't want to have to move our camp every time we fire our guns. Now that the rabbit is stored away we'll go hunting south of here."

They ate another Clif Bar, and some leftover Spam from supper the night before. They then headed south down the hillside to find a good spot to hunt another 3,000 paces from their camp. They carefully traveled down the slope stepping over fallen trees and avoiding the sting of branches as they walked under the thick pine canopy. They arrived at the bottom of the hill only to stumble out into a wide clearing. Cobie dragged her daughter back into the woods quickly.

Cobie looked up and down the clearing and saw overhead electrical wires, a road on the far side of the clearing and several deer about 300 yards away down the left side of the clearing.

"Baby girl we'll stick to this side of the woods until the clearing narrows just after the bend of the road. Follow me."

Cobie walked another 200 yards in the shadows of the trees before they crossed the clearing and dropped behind a fallen tree to see if anyone was following them. They started walking toward where Cobie saw the deer when they heard a rifle shot. Cobie dropped to her knees and pulled her binoculars out to see where the shot came from. She saw a man, woman, and a young girl dragging one of the deer into the woods.

"Darn, they shot my deer."

"Let me see," Cloe said just as two more shots rang out from further east and the man fell to the ground.

Cobie grabbed the binoculars back and saw the woman drop to the ground to check on her husband as a young man ran up with a rifle looking for who shot the man. Another shot rang out, the young man's head exploded into a red mist, and his body jerked to the ground causing the woman to scream.

Cobie and Cloe were about 25 yards away, so the sound was muffled as they scrambled behind several fallen trees to watch what was happening. They heard the sound of engines coming toward them from the west and kept low, while the men parked their strange-looking military styled vehicles and walked over to the people with guns drawn. The woman raised a pistol up to shoot one of the men, and another slapped it from her hands. The second man backhanded the woman sending her to the ground.

"Praise Allah, you saved my life. This is another sign from Allah that the Demon shall be crushed."

"The hundred dead infidels back in Medford and Ashland are a testament to Allah's will. We will keep raiding the towns until the entirety of our enemies is dead. Their government is powerless to stop us."

"Praise Allah, it shall be done."

"Allahu Akbar!"

One of the men tied the woman and girl's hands behind them and shoved them to the ground. The men examined the stranger's guns and tossed them aside. One of the men spat on the dead deer and kicked it before they turned to the women. Another man made the woman stand and then ripped her clothes off her body. Cobie covered Cloe's eyes and turned her head from the horrible scene when suddenly the woman screamed as one of the men turned his attention to the young girl. The man raping the woman hit her on the side of her head with his fist, and she stopped screaming. The men finished their debauchery, loaded the woman and girl into the larger vehicle, and drove east staying in the clearing until they were out of sight.

Cloe cried, then got mad and said, "Those men killed the father and son and then raped the mother and daughter. We need to kill them. Were they Islamic? Those were the same words terrorists use when they kill people."

"Dear, calm down. We can't fight men that have AK47s and military vehicles with machine guns. I think they were from the Middle East, but we can't worry about that now; we need to butcher that deer and take anything that will help us survive. Save your crying, and we can both fall apart when we get that meat back to our camp. Suck it up and follow me," Cobie said as she gently massaged her crying daughter's shoulders.

***

Joe was out after lunch exploring the eastern side of his property hunting when he spotted several deer heading east through the woods. He hadn't seen any deer so far so he decided he would follow them until he could get a clean kill. He knew he was at least a mile due east of his property when he lost the deer and began tracking them. He came to an extensive clearing that cut through the forest for power line right a ways when he saw the deer in a clearing ahead. He hated to shoot and field dress a deer so far from home because he couldn't carry all of the meat.

He silently got closer to the grazing deer when a gunshot rang out, and one of the deer dropped to the ground. Joe fell to the ground and hid when he saw the family run out to claim his deer. Even though they shot the deer away from his property, he was pissed because he had tracked the deer from his property for miles. He wanted half of that deer but decided to remain hidden from everyone.

He watched as the man prepared to butcher the deer when several shots cracked from a long way off and the man dropped to the ground. He was revolted as the scene played out and the two women were thrown into the odd vehicles. He thought about shooting the men but there were five of them, and one stayed in the larger vehicle and manned the machine gun on top. He felt powerless but decided he would at least get fresh deer meat at these other poor soul's expense. Joe was too far away to hear what the men said and guessed they were arguing over the women.

The vehicles sped off heading east, and Joe carefully walked toward the deer and two dead men when he heard a stick snap in the woods to his left. He dropped prone to the ground and waited to see if the men left someone behind to mop up the area. He saw two figures crawling to the deer and then stand as they watched the eastern horizon for the attackers. The pair pulled out knives, cut the two hindquarters from the deer, and placed them in cloth bags. Then they searched the area and took two rifles, a pistol, and several other items from the dead men. They took one of the men's backpack and loaded it with their booty, slung the bags over their shoulders and turned toward him to leave.

Joe gasped and said to himself, "It's that beautiful woman from Cobb's Outfitters. She must have a cabin nearby the lake."

He watched as the two women left with half of his deer. He wanted to catch her attention and see how they were doing since the crap hit the fan. He forced himself to stay hidden because the two women could be part of a larger group. She was beautiful, but he didn't dare expose himself to possible danger. He watched the two small women struggle to carry the extra weight and followed them after he cut the front haunches from the deer and slung them over his shoulder. They made so much noise he could have been driving an army tank behind them, and they only looked back twice as he followed them from a distance.

The women stopped to rest, and he inched close enough to hear their conversation, "Baby girl, I'm sorry that you had to be exposed to that horrible cruelty back there. I hate those men, and if given a chance I will kill them, but I can't risk endangering you. We have to concentrate on surviving ourselves, and I think that means staying hidden from others."

"Mom, we could sneak up on them and kill them before they know we are there."

"Darling, suppose we do that and twenty men come to find the others. These men were killers and not just in the woods surviving. They spat on the deer. They didn't need the deer because they are well supplied. I don't know who they are, but they are our enemies and enemies of our country," the woman told the young girl.

The women were rested and headed up a steep hill until they arrived at their camp. Since they weren't making noise, Joe slowed and stopped about 50 yards from their camp to listen in on their conversation. This obviously wasn't their home, and he wanted to know where their home was and how far away it was from him. He then remembered her conversation with the man at the store and her saying something about being evicted. He wondered if she was just squatting out in the forest when the bombs dropped.

***

"Cloe, walk Bennie so he can do his business away from our camp. Don't go out of sight and take your guns with you while I cut off some of the deer for our supper and pack the rest in the snow."

Cloe took the muzzle from Bennie, untied her dog from a tree, and began walking sideways across the hillside toward Joe. Bennie barked once, and Cloe admonished him to be quiet. He knew he couldn't leave his position without alerting the young girl so thinking quickly he cut a small piece of meat from the deer haunch and pitched it away from him for the dog to find. Bennie caught the smell and drug Cloe toward the meat. The two made enough sound to cover Joe's retreat away from the women's camp.

Cobie waited until dark and made a fire to roast several pounds of the venison by holding strips of the meat over the flame, as one would roast hotdogs. The first batch was overcooked, but they ate it like ravenous wolves tearing apart an unlucky animal. They each ate over a pound of the cooked meat and gave Bennie the scraps. Their faces and hands were greasy from their meal, but their stomachs were full, and their eyes grew weary.

"We'll head home in the morning since we have all of the meat and guns we can carry. I hated for those poor people to run out of luck, but we now have a decent Remington 30.06, a Winchester 30.30 lever action, a Glock 17 9mm pistol and almost 50 bullets for each. Baby girl, I don't know if I could have gotten close enough to drop a deer with the slugs. These deer rifles may save our lives. You take the 30.30, and my .380 and I'll take the 30.06 and the 9mm pistol," said Cobie to a very drowsy young girl.

Cloe woke up the next morning and found her mother had everything ready to go. She also saw a weird looking set of bags tied together beside the dead campfire. They ate cold venison left over from the night before, and Cobie placed the odd bags on Bennie's back and strapped them in place.

"Bennie has been promoted to pack mule. He's a big dog, but I'm starting him with lightweight packs so he can get used to carrying a load. It will help us get back to the cabin without having to rest so much."

☆

Chapter 7

Joe left the women behind and headed back to the cabin taking a northern route while being careful to leave as few signs of his passing as possible. He doubled back on his trail every half mile and watched for anyone following him. He thought he heard faint voices several times but never saw anyone. He was a half-mile north of his property and a mile east of his cabin when he saw the first group of people heading into the mountains. He hid and watched as two families scurried in the valley below heading north along an old

Forestry Service road. They were walking very fast as though someone or something was following them.

Joe stayed in his hiding spot for another ten minutes before stretching his legs to head on home when he heard voices again.

"Babe, we can't stop, or those men will catch up to us."

"Mike, I told you twice that I think they drove this way into the mountains when they left Ashland. We could be walking right into them. They killed all those people and wouldn't hesitate to kill us, either."

"I know what I'm doing let's head on up in the mountains and hope we find an abandoned cabin."

"I want to stop here," the woman said.

Joe heard them and decided to take action. He shook the tree limbs above him then stomped the ground as he moved toward them. Then he yelled, "I see them. Shoot the man, and we'll take the girl."

They took off heading northeast along the Forest Service road and were soon out of sight.

Joe laughed, but that was all he had to hear to put a fire under his own butt and get moving back to his new home. Before he cut back down to his property, he saw two more families heading higher into the mountains and wondered if the men who killed the two men back in that clearing were the same men who these people were running from.

He was only a short distance from the cabin when he heard some thrashing up ahead. He saw a woman making camp by the creek close to his cabin. He stopped and watched as she sat on her coat crying. Her face was dirty, and her clothes were ripped in several places. He could tell she was a beautiful blonde about 30 years old and didn't have a clue about surviving in the woods. She had a short skirt on with a tight white blouse and designer shoes not fit for walking.

The woman looked in her bag, looked disgusted, and started crying uncontrollably. Joe stood there watching the beauty from the bank above her when suddenly his foot slipped, and he tumbled down the hill toward her. The woman was terrified by the sudden appearance of the stranger and waved a knife at him.

He stopped a few feet from her flat on his back and said, "Good afternoon. Put the knife down. I mean you no harm. You are on private property and need to move on."

The woman stood up and walked over to Joe who was still flat on his back trying to catch his wind, "Please help me, I'm starving. I will do anything for you if you will give me food. I can work for you. Cook for you. Hell, I'll even sleep with you for food."

"Whoa, lady. Back up for a minute," Joe said as he scampered to his feet then added, "Where are you from, and why are you on my property?"

"Those terrorists killed my husband, the entire Ashland City Council, and the police. We thought they were FEMA coming to help us. Until this attack, my worst worry was how to direct the help at the country club to decorate for the next social event or if we should travel to Paris or Cancun for our trip that month. Please help me."

"Why did they kill your husband?"

"My husband tried to reason with them. He was the county prosecutor and from a wealthy family. Those men didn't even listen to him. They shot him down like a dog, and they rounded up everyone they could find and executed them in front of City Hall. They only kept a few of the women for their ... uh ... entertainment. I'm starving. Do you have any food?" the lady begged.

Joe asked, "What's your name and how did you escape?"

She smiled, "My name is Madison Clark, and I escaped when the men I was with stopped the vehicle we were riding in to sample the captured women. While the three men were doing disgusting things to those poor women, I ran into the woods and kept running. Now I'm here with my knight in shining armor sent to rescue me from the terrorist."

Joe frowned at her fishy story and asked, "Why do you keep saying they are terrorists?"

"Because they spoke in a weird language and kept saying Aly Akber or something like the terrorists always say before they blow themselves up on the news."

Joe was now in a quandary because he wanted to help the poor woman but didn't want her to know where he lived so to give him time to think he said, "I'm out hunting for several days and will take you back to my place when I finish hunting. Here take these energy bars and this can of Spam to fill you up until I can cook tonight. We can't have a fire during the day, or someone might see the smoke."

The woman wolfed the food down quickly as Joe figured out what to do. He gave her his blanket and told her he was going to finish hunting for the day and would be back before dark. Joe quickly arrived at his cabin and packed the venison in the snow that he carried in from the back of the cabin. He then gathered his sleeping bag and enough camping gear to fool the lady. At the last minute, he filled a bag with stuff to place about the old ramshackle cabin to make it look like he lived there. The old broken-down cabin was filthy but would work nicely since he didn't want the woman to stay with him long term. He made the cabin look like he had been there for a while and then left to join her back at the creek.

"I'm scared. I'm so glad you came back here for me. You are so strong, and I just know you will protect me."

Joe wasn't buying her story but couldn't figure out what her game was besides getting her belly full, so he played along. He started a small fire and cooked Spam along with a can of green beans and some stale crackers. He didn't want the lady to become too comfortable or like the food too much. They ate as Madison kept talking about her luxurious life in Ashland and her high society life before the shit hit the fan.

She noticed Joe wasn't paying much attention to her constant blabbing and became silent for a few minutes then said, "Joe do you have a wife or girlfriend back at your place?"

Joe knew where this was heading and replied, "No and I don't need one either. I lived alone before the attack and will live alone after you move on. I'll help you and then send you on your way. It wouldn't be Christian to let you starve. Look, lady, I don't have a big store of food, and I have to hunt every day just to feed myself. I would have to hunt twice as much to feed you also, and there just aren't enough hours in the day to do everything that must be done."

The woman smiled back at Joe convinced even more that this simple guy could be molded into being her provider, protector, and lover until she could find a more prosperous and powerful man. She had never worked a day in her life, and all of her riches were gained by sleeping her way up the social ladder until she found the right rich man. Even in the apocalypse, the woman schemed to start with Joe and keep working her assets until she wound up at the top again.

That night Joe gave the woman two blankets and told her to curl up close to the campfire to keep warm. Joe settled down in his cozy subzero-sleeping bag and slept soundly. He woke up before dawn with a naked Madison curled up in his sleeping bag against his back. It took considerable effort on his part to not shuck his clothes and give in to this temptress. He went back to sleep with Madison trying to get his attention. He slapped her hand, and she stopped moving.

Joe slid out of the sleeping bag waking Madison who begged him to come back and spend the morning with her.

Joe replied, "Sorry but I have to go hunting this morning, and you need to clean up the camp and pack our gear, I'll be back in three to four hours. Be ready to travel."

He left the sleepy woman at the makeshift camp wrapped up in his sleeping bag and headed to the oldest broken-down cabin. Joe repaired the front door, boarded over a couple of broken windows, and cleaned up a bit. He then made a couple more trips between his home and the old cabin and thought he was now ready to take the woman to his fake home.

He stuffed two of his Grandma's letters in his coat pocket and read one before heading back to the camp. It read:

Dear Joe:

It should be mid-winter at your new home in the woods. Remember to keep dry and stay as warm as possible in the bone chilling Oregon winters. Layer your clothes since what feels good in the morning will make you sweat in the afternoon. If you ever fall into the water and get wet make sure you dry yourself and get warm as soon as possible. Start a fire if you can. If not get naked with someone and share a sleeping bag. A woman would be nice but don't let the ick factor keep you from getting warm. A man's body will also keep you warm."

Love Grandma.

Joe found that he was talking to himself again, "Now that was weird timing with Madison naked in my sleeping bag. Grandma is looking down from above."

He walked up to Madison and expected her ready to leave but found her snuggled up in his sleeping bag with none of the tasks completed. He quickly packed up his possessions and used his toe to nudge her butt until she woke up.

"Wake up. It's after 10 am. Get your butt up Madison. We need to go," a disgusted Joe said firmly.

Madison poked her head out of Joe's sleeping bag and said, "Where is the coffee? I need coffee to get going."

"Get your butt up, or I will leave you here in the woods. I'm leaving in ten minutes whether you come or not."

She stood up without any clothes on; put her blouse and skirt on while making sure Joe was looking at her naked body as she dressed. Then she put her shoes and jacket on as she shivered while she walked behind a large bush for a few minutes then came back.

"Joe, I want to be your friend, and we could live together and make a good life for both of us," Madison said as she wrapped her arms around Joe and tried to kiss him.

Joe moved away and replied, "I'm sure there will be some man who will be glad to take care of you and make you his wife. That man is not standing here. I just want to get your strength up and send you on your way. I'll look for a family walking through that needs a woman to join them."

This made her mad, and she walked away from Joe as he turned and walked away. He made a wide circle back to the old cabin. It only took a minute before she was on his heels following him like a puppy dog. He walked her in circles for two hours before heading to the dilapidated cabin from the south.

They arrived at the broken-down cabin, and Joe said, "Well, it ain't much, but it's home."

Madison's lip curled, and her nose headed skyward as she showed contempt for the old cabin.

Joe saw her face turn red and her fingers turn white as she gripped his arm, "Hey, what were you expecting? Like you, I had to flee from the chaos and find a place to hide until those criminals and crazy people killed each other. It's dry and will keep a bear out. Get used to it or go find a better place."

Madison smiled as she said, "I'm sorry Joe, but it's far from what I'm used to but, we can make a home of it until it's safe back in the city. I'm sorry that I've acted childish and like a spoiled brat, but I do appreciate what you have done to survive, and you are a good man to have taken me in and fed me. Thank you."

Joe stammered, and she could see him soften as he said, "I'm sorry for being a hardass, but I just want to live alone in peace and enjoy the woods around me. I'll try to play nice."

Madison tried to give him a kiss on the cheek, but he ducked. She knew she was close to setting the hook. She had also learned to play nice and tried harder to fit in with this overweight but very handsome man. She knew the key to his heart was through good cooking, acting like a pioneer woman, and great sex. She knew she had the cooking and sex parts nailed; she just had to act as if she were a pioneer lady to win his heart.

"What do we have for food? Let me cook a nice supper for a hardworking man," she said as she ran her fingers through his hair.

Madison looked at the kitchen then said, "I have to clean this up a bit before I can cook on that old wood stove."

It only took an hour for her to wipe down the kitchen counter, table, and stove before preparing supper. Joe brought in some kindling, a pile of wood for the stove, and built a hot fire before going outside to set some trip wires and a couple of snares for rabbits.

Madison cleaned herself up, combed her hair, and did the best she could to look good for Joe when he came in to eat. She looked at herself in a small mirror she found on a shelf and saw a beautiful face dressed in torn dirty clothing. It was the best she could do until she could talk Joe into going to town to do some shopping. There wasn't much to work with, so she fried two venison steaks, made instant mashed potatoes and corn for their supper. When the steaks were done, she opened the door in time to see Joe sit down on the porch to take his boots off. She scurried over in front of him, helped pull his boots off, and placed them just inside the door.

She sat down on the steps with Joe, "I wish I could hand you your favorite cocktail or beer after a long day's work. You deserve a stiff drink today after putting up with me and hunting for two days. I'm sorry about my behavior I was starving and desperate. I've had an easy life and never went hungry or wanted for anything in my life. I have to adapt quickly. Could you teach me the skills I need to survive?"

"I'm starving. We'll discuss that after supper. Before we go inside, I want you to know that I understand that being a female alone with all the crap flying is a scary thing. Just be honest with me and don't try to deceive me and we'll get along," Joe replied.

The meal was good, and Joe liked the pan-fried venison better than roasted over a direct fire. They had a good discussion concerning what had happened in the world, and Joe filled her in on what he had heard on the radio. Madison then steered the conversation to how could she better equip herself with the knowledge to survive.

"Joe, I've always used my charm and other assets to make my way in the world. I started out in a poor family and wrangled my way into a great prep school and then a good college just so I could meet a rich and powerful man so I could live the good life. I'm not ashamed of what I did or what I was. Since this war started, I have done some soul-searching and have to adapt to my new environment and do what it takes to

92

survive," Madison shared much more than Joe ever thought she would.

"I'll be glad to help you with the little I know about surviving. I know a lot about hunting, fishing, and camping but not a lot of warfare and defending myself. I'll teach you what I know. So does that mean you will stop using your charm on me to get your way," Joe ended with a laugh.

"Thanks very much for offering the training and I will help do chores or whatever you need for me to do around here. Now about me using my charm and assets to get my way, well, I guess that's just built into me. You will just have to resist my charms and assets the best way you can," she replied as she scrapped the plates and placed them in the dry sink to wash.

Joe started to get up from the table when Madison said, "Joe could you find something to do for about half an hour after I get the dishes done? I saw that large wash tub out on the back porch, and I think I'll fit into it. I want to take a hot bath or at least clean up a bit if you'll haul some water up to the cabin so I can heat it to wash my clothes and me. Do you have an old t-shirt I can wear, until my clothes dry in the morning?"

"Why yes, I have to skin a couple of rabbits and a couple of other chores to do myself," he said as he sniffed his underarm and added, "I need a bath myself. I think living alone is not a great for personal hygiene. I haven't had a full bath since the shit hit the fan. Oh, I have a couple of shirts and a spare pair of pants if you want them."

Joe hauled two five-gallon buckets from the creek to the kitchen and Madison placed a bucket full on the old cook stove to heat up for her bath. He brought the big washtub into the kitchen then went back outside to get his chores done. He skinned the rabbits, cut both of the deer haunches into steaks, and saved the fat to use for frying food and then gathered firewood until Madison called for him to come in the cabin.

She only had his t-shirt on as she sat on an old stool drying her hair by the fire. Her beauty was stunning against the light from the fire, and he made himself look away as she turned toward him with her long bare legs pointing toward him.

"Joe, I'll go in the bedroom if you want to take a bath. We can leave the door open, so I get some heat. I promise not to peek," She said with a mischievous grin on her face.

"I think I'll take you up on that. Washing out of a bucket is better than nothing but a good hot tub bath is much better," he said as he placed a bucket of water on the stove to heat.

Madison replied, "Here, I'll help you empty the water and fetch clean water for your bath."

"I'll just use your water. It looks pretty clear to me, and frankly, I'm too tired to lug the water, "Joe answered.

"Are you sure? I hate for you to use my dirty water," she said very sincerely.

"Madison, if that's the worst I have to do to stay reasonably clean then I'm a fortunate man to take a bath after a beautiful woman." Joe was smiling then quickly frowned when he realized he was flirting back with her.

Joe poured the hot water in the tub and Madison left for the bedroom. Joe stripped down and soaked for several minutes in the soothing water before he began scrubbing two weeks' worth of dirt off his body. He finished his bath and then dropped his clothes in the tub to wash them. He put on his spare clothes and said, "Madison, I'm dressed now. You can come back in the room."

She didn't answer so he poked his head into the room and saw she was sound asleep in the middle of the only bed in the cabin. He had planned for them to both share the bed, but he would sleep in his sleeping bag. The couch was actually an ancient futon that was crappy at best. He tried sleeping on the futon and found it so lumpy it killed his back, so he placed his sleeping bag on the floor in front of the fire and went to sleep.

About midnight Madison woke up and didn't see Joe, so she got up and walked into the living room and saw him on the floor still awake.

"Joe, get up and come to bed. I'll stay on my side and won't attack you."

"Okay, you fell asleep in the middle of the bed, and I didn't want to disturb you," Joe said as he gathered his sleeping bag and joined her on the bed.

Joe woke up in the morning spooning Madison with her head resting on his arm and his other around her waist. He lay there thinking two weeks ago, she was a happily married rich woman without a care in the world, and five weeks ago, he was getting married to his high school sweetheart. It then dawned on him that this woman could teach survival lessons to the Special Forces. She had tried wiggling her assets at him to no avail then switched to the helpless girl who wanted to learn from the big strong man.

Joe liked the thought of a beautiful warm body next to him in the morning; however, he was pissed about this woman's tactics. He was not in the frame of mind to be manipulated ever again.

He lay there for over an hour thinking about how to proceed with Madison's training and how much to let her know about his real situation. He knew she would use him to get what she wanted so he convinced himself that her companionship and help around the cabin would make it worth his effort.

Joe felt her stir and played possum until he heard her close the bathroom door. He jumped out of bed, dressed, and quickly placed several logs on the fire. He stirred the embers until he had the fire going again.

He looked outside and saw there was a new carpet of white snow on the ground. This frightened him because someone could easily track them if they went hunting with snow on the ground. He needed to go back to the other cabin to check on it and bring some more food back but didn't want to take the risk.

"Madison, we need to stay close to the cabin today due to the fresh snow outside. Normally I'd be hunting since it's easy to track animals in the snow, but it's also easy to track humans, and I'm worried about people walking through the area and some bad guys that drove through here a couple of days ago. I think they are the same people that killed your husband and kidnapped you and the other women," Joe informed Madison.

"Well, it's not all that bad; I see a deck of cards on the shelf along with a couple of board games. You could even teach me some survival skills while we're stuck in our home," she smiled.

Joe caught the crap about our home, and it made him mad that she thought he was dumb or horny enough to buy everything she said.

He thought for a minute and replied, "That's a good idea. We can train you how to set rabbit traps and then how to skin and gut what we catch. We can even build a rough smoker and smoke the meat at night."

He gloated when the smile washed off her pretty face, but then she cheerfully said, "That sounds yucky to me, but I want to contribute and not be a drag on you so I'll kick myself in the butt and do what you tell me to do. Let's get after it once I warm up some leftover venison for breakfast."

"Okay, that works for me. I have a couple of things to do while you fix breakfast."

Joe took another letter from his coat pocket and began to read.

Dear Joe:

I know you are a good person because I spent so much time with you during your formative years and our weekly chats. Don't become jaded because she fooled around with your best friend. Life is a bitch, and sometimes you have to laugh and move on. You will find the love of your life one day, and she will be faithful to you. Don't settle for anyone that comes along, be picky and don't settle for less than you deserve. You will know she's the one when you think about her every day and can't live without her and she feels the same way about you.

I hope my letters are as helpful to you as they were to me. Oh, yes I did have to add several notes after I heard about the Explorer incident. Karma is great. You need to forgive those two and thank God, your friend took that cheating bitch from you before she took half of what you own in a divorce. LOL

Love Grandma.

Joe felt someone behind him and caught Madison staring over his shoulder, "Joe what are you reading? You were laughing, and it caught my interest."

"My Grandma died a few weeks back, and we were very close. She left me a series of letters to open over the next two years along with the land you are standing on. I just wish she'd left me a mansion with a good furnace," he laughed.

Madison said, "She must have been a very special woman."

"She was very special to my Dad and me. We were the closest to her, in the family, and I miss her every day. The letters help soften the grief of losing her. Now that the world has turned upside down the letters help me muddle through the day," he said with a tear running down his cheek.

Joe opened the door to see it was snowing and walked out of the cabin to fetch more firewood when he was surprised by Bennie jumping on him.

"Hey big boy, how are you doing?"

Joe petted Bennie and scratched behind his ears. Bennie ran to the front of the cabin where Joe found a dead rabbit. Bennie had brought a present to Joe that morning and then ran away back home. Joe watched him disappear into the woods thinking about the woman with the black hair. Then he noticed something that scared the crap out of him. The dog was leaving tracks everywhere he went.

The snow quickly covered the tracks, so there wasn't any danger today, but he was concerned the dog might lead the wrong people to his door.

☆

Chapter 8

A few days later, the weather had warmed, and the snow had melted. Joe had to get out of the cabin and clear his head. Madison hoovered around Joe trying her best to get him interested in her until he was so fed up he just had to escape.

"Madison, I'll be gone for a while," Joe said as he packed his backpack and rolled up his sleeping bag.

"Honey, where are you going?"

"I need to run my traps and check to make sure there are no intruders nearby. Don't worry if I'm gone overnight. Sometimes crap happens, and I have to camp out," Joe said as he walked to the door.

"But Joe, I planned on a special evening for us."

"It will have to wait," he said as he marched out the door and into the woods.

Joe power walked into the woods and didn't look back at the cabin. His leg muscles burned from the increased walking. He had thought he was in good shape for a fat boy but walking everywhere was kicking his butt. He trudged on knowing that the exercise was good for him and he would eventually get used to it. He hoped.

He finally stopped and took a deep breath to clear his head. The constant talking, flirting and smothering from Madison told him all he wanted to know about her. He already knew she wasn't for him, but he couldn't stand her enough to keep her around for friends with benefits. She was just too needy and would be as bossy as Gwen would have been if he allowed her to get comfortable. He was determined to get rid of her when the time was right.

He walked around for a while and found himself northeast of his property in the woods looking out at the quarry. The quarry hadn't been in operation for a few years and had been abandoned. He searched the machine sheds for anything useful and found nothing. He moved on to the office and found someone was using the building for shelter. He saw blankets, candles, and a few canned goods. He quickly left without disturbing anything.

Joe checked his map and compass and walked northeast cross-country to Dead Indian Road. He wanted to get on Dead Indian Road above the businesses that were northwest of town. He remembered there was a couple of companies and several beautiful homes along the road toward town. The walk was strenuous, but he enjoyed being out of the cabin and away from Madison. He felt he could breathe again now that she wasn't hovering around him. Then he thought, *she did feel very warm and sexy this morning in bed.*

Joe had to take a short break after the trek up and down the hills to get to the highway, so he hid in some bushes beside the road. He rested only a few minutes when he heard a vehicle approaching but lost the sound when it turned off the road below him. Joe knew that he had to stay hidden because even good people would turn bad and kill if they thought it would help them survive.

After fifteen minutes, he shouldered his backpack and crossed the highway to scout out the business across the road. The company was abandoned as most were so he surveilled the buildings and parking lots for movement before entering the first building. The company had been a welding shop that catered to the lumber business.

Joe only found a small bag full of tools and a little roll of small diameter wire to take with him from the production building. He then searched the office and found a bottle of Wild Turkey, a few bottles of water and a vending machine full of candy bars and chips. He broke the glass and ate his fill of potato chips and candy bars before loading his booty into his carry bag, which he unfolded from his backpack.

He started to walk away from the shop when he looked back and saw the six new cars and trucks Joe had snubbed his nose at and bypassed because he knew they wouldn't start. He opened the door of a new Ford pickup, searched the glove box, the console, and lifted the clamshell cover for treasure. He only found a set of golf clubs in the back of the truck and took a nine iron to use as a walking stick.

The next vehicle was a red 2032 Corvette that was locked. Joe looked at the Nine Iron, then the Corvette, and then clubbed the passenger side window to gain entrance. He found a lady's overnight bag full of lingerie and makeup. He spilled the contents on the driver's side floorboard and leaned into the car to gather the dropped items when he saw the Ruger LCP in a little holster strapped to the bottom of the seat. He felt on under the seat and found a box of .38 Special bullets for the gun. He tucked the pistol in his waistband and placed the box of shells into his coat pocket.

He finished searching all the vehicles and added two excellent hunting knives, a small backpack, and three car magazines to his growing bag of goodies. He walked around to the back of the business and saw a side road that came up behind the houses fronting Dead Indian Road. He tried to keep hidden in the bushes alongside the road, but there was an open stretch before the first house. Joe didn't want to be seen, so he left his carry bag and tool bag in the ditch beside the road and crawled into the ditch to get past the open spot undetected.

He slipped out of the ditch when he was able to use a tree to block anyone in the house from seeing him. Again, he watched the house and yard for any signs of danger before proceeding into the backyard. The house had a huge attached garage, swimming pool, and pool house in the backyard, so he started his hunt there. He would have loved to take a swim, but the water was icy cold and full of slimy green algae.

The door to the pool house was locked, so Joe jimmied the lock with a pry bar taken from his new tool bag. The door popped open, but there was nothing of interest in the house.

The garage had several expensive cars and motorcycles that were new but wouldn't run. What interested Joe was a nice older Jeep Rubicon parked by a well-equipped shop. He got in the Jeep, found a key, and it started right up. Joe quickly shut the engine down, and since Joe's backpack and carry bag were full, he loaded them all into the jeep. He would search this house, and the next then make a mad dash back to his cabin. He would hide the Jeep in the forest close to his property but not so close people would find him. He nosed around the small workshop and threw some more tools, cans of oil, and a spare gas can into the back seat. The jeep was full of gas and had a jerry can mounted on the back bumper, which was full.

He watched his surroundings carefully as he moved to the back door and jimmied it open. He found a horrible mess in the house, which had been looted and abused. The house stunk, and he covered his face with a wet handkerchief.

"Damn, this place smells like shit. Human shit at that," Joe said as the raunchy smell attacked his nose and lungs.

Looters had not only taken what they wanted but knocked holes in the walls and spray painted graffiti nearly everywhere. He did find several bottles of antibiotics and nonprescription pain relievers in the upstairs bathroom that had been tossed on the floor. These looters wanted hard drugs and food. They tore the place up and literally crapped on the floors. He went into one of the bedrooms and selected a variety of women's clothes that looked to be Madison's size and stuffed them in a pillowcase. He threw in some toiletries and a pair of women's boots and then continued his search.

He decided he would only search the next house before returning to the cabin. He had thought about Madison as he searched the house and a beautiful warm body and female companionship were winning out over her poor behavior. He would return and have a frank discussion with Madison. He would set boundaries and expectation on her behavior if she wanted to stay with him.

Joe cut across a field of tall grass to the next house, which was similar to the one he'd just left. It was a large, expensive house with a pool and a five-car garage. Joe searched the garage with zero success and moved into the house. The backdoor was open, and he found the same mess. The strange thing that hit him was that the place looked too trashed and didn't stink. He walked to the front door and saw it had been forcibly opened, but the lock was intact. He walked into the kitchen, rummaged through the cabinets, and saw a few cans of beans and canned tomatoes but not much to eat.

Joe searched each room, and then it dawned on him that while things were broken, the house and furnishings were not broken. Trash was piled on them. He knocked the newspapers, torn drapes, and empty vegetable cans from the couch and it didn't have a stain. He used the toe of his boot to nudge a pile of crap and wasn't surprised that it turned out to be fake. The opened vegetable cans were clean inside. Now he smelled a rat.

Then it all came together. The place was staged, and the people that lived here were probably still here and hiding. He walked through the house again and saw the closet under the stairs. He had opened the door and looked in the closet before but only saw a few coats hanging with stacks of boxes and books behind them. Joe shoved the coats out of the way and tried to lift a box of the books and found the box wouldn't move. He took his flashlight from his shirt pocket, examined the wall behind the boxes, and discovered the wall was a doorway.

Joe tugged and pulled on the boxes and books until he heard a latch click. He pulled the boxes to him, and the wall opened like a door on hinges. He looked into the dark room behind the fake wall to see a room about the size of a bedroom. There was a bed, sleeping bags, and boxes of food to his right and a small table and chairs to his left.

He saw a slight movement and then saw the woman and two kids behind the food boxes when he shined his flashlight from above them.

"Mister, please don't hurt my kids. I'll do anything you want but don't hurt my kids. Take our food and leave us alone," the frightened woman said.

The kids stopped crying when Joe said in a very calm voice, "Lady, I'm not here to hurt you or the kids. I won't take your food. I thought I was searching an abandoned home. You need to make the place look dirty, so others won't find you. You did a good job making the place look looted, but it's too clean. The house next door has human crap on the floor, and everything is covered in filth."

"Then go away and leave us alone," the woman said.

"Is there anything I can do for you? Is your husband here," Joe asked?

"These are my grandkids. I was babysitting while they were visiting friends up in Portland. My son will be back soon," the woman said in an unsteady voice.

Joe asked, "Do you have a gun?"

"I do at my home in Medford, but my daughter in law is one of those anti-gun nuts and won't allow them in her house. I feel naked without one."

"Here take this pistol and box of bullets. I found them today and don't need them," Joe said as he handed the gun and bullets to her.

"Thanks. Have you seen any police or people around out there?"

"Lady, the good people are hunkered down. There are plenty of bad men and women burning and looting. I see a new large fire in town and over toward Medford every time I look. I'm leaving now. Stay hidden as long as possible and perhaps the crazies will move on," Joe said.

Joe opened the garage door and backed the Jeep out on to the driveway as he watched for trouble. He sped down the back road stopping just long enough to gather his bag and tools. He made the turn off to Dead Indian Road and headed up the access road that went back to his property. He passed the old quarry and doubled back quickly to see if it would make a great hiding spot for the Jeep.

One of the equipment sheds backed up to the massive hill behind it. There was just enough room to drive the Jeep behind the shed. He took his bags out of the Jeep, parked it behind the shed, and covered it with brush. Upon exiting the Jeep, he raised the hood and removed the battery cables, which he placed in his bag.

The bags were heavy, but he quickly covered the two miles back to the cabin where he found Madison cleaning the inside from top to bottom. She only had a t-shirt on, and every time she raised her arms above her head, he saw what had made him temper his thoughts about running her off. Joe slapped himself and walked around to the front of the cabin. He stomped his feet loud enough to alert Madison and dropped the bags on the porch.

A minute later Madison came through the door wearing her skirt on over the t-shirt. She was barefooted but helped him take his boots off

"I'm sorry I have been too clingy. I'm so sorry, but I have been scared to death since this crap happened. I promise not to bother you, and I will work my ass off to help you. Just tell me what to do, and I will do it to make your burden lighter," Madison said with tears in her eyes.

Joe stood up, pulled her close, and hugged her. "Madison, I'm also sorry. I just suffered a terrible tragedy where my fiancee and best friend died on the same day and lost my Grandma a short while later. I took my anger out on you and will do better in the future. Be yourself and don't try to play me and we'll get along just fine. Oh, I brought some things home that you need."

"Hon, we'll look at them later. You look exhausted and need to sit down and prop your feet up by the fireplace. I'll have supper ready for you when you are rested up a bit. I wish I had a Bourbon and coke to share with you," she said with a laugh.

Joe reached into one of the bags and brought out the Wild Turkey and said, "Pour us a stiff one and sit beside me on the couch so we can relax for a minute."

The drink was what Joe needed, and he filled Madison on every detail of his trip. She put supper on the table, and Joe ate as if he'd not seen food for a month. He helped her clean up after supper, and then they both sat on the couch and had another glass of Bourbon.

"Madison, I thought about you quite a bit while I was gone and got these for you," he said as he handed her the pillowcase.

She smiled when she pulled out the winter boots and the clothes but jumped with joy when she pulled out the panties and bras. She held up a pair of French cut panties and kissed Joe on the cheek.

"Joe, I've had to wear the same pair since the crap hit the fan. I have to go commando while they dry each day. Thank you so much for thinking of me," she said before pulling his head to her and giving him a long hot kiss.

Joe pulled a black thong from his pocket and said, "See I was thinking of you."

Madison stood up, dropped her skirt to the floor, and lifted her t-shirt above her head exposing her naked body. She took the thong, stepped her long legs into them, and drew them slowly up her legs while Joe watched with an open mouth. She moved to him and straddled his lap as she smothered him in kisses. She unbuttoned his shirt and then unfastened his belt in a fever as they writhed in heated passion. They were soon naked on the couch making love for the first time of many times that night.

☆

Chapter 9

The early spring weather warmed suddenly during the night, and Cobie woke up to the sound of rain hitting the tin roof. She thought the sound was beautiful because it meant spring wasn't too far away. She noticed a noise coming from the inside of the cabin that sounded like water splashing and jumped out of bed to run to the kitchen. There were several steady drops of water hitting the floor in every room. Cobie grabbed buckets and pans and placed them below the drips to catch the water. Now the dripping noise sounded like a symphony of musicians playing out of sync.

Cobie lay down in her warm sleeping bag but could not go to sleep until the constant drumming noise from the rain on the tin roof lulled her back to sleep. When she woke up the snow was gone, and it was 45 degrees outside and sunny. Cobie and her daughter made the most of the warm weather. They shucked their parkas and Cobie took Cloe hunting after being cooped up in the cabin for several days. Cobie knew that the men that killed those people could easily track them in the snow. They had stayed in the cabin playing games during the daylight hours and smoking meat in a makeshift smoker inside the hearth. Now the rain had melted the snow, and they could venture out.

"Mom let's try heading west today for our hunt. We ran into those killers southeast of here," her daughter said.

"It's worth a try. We need to be careful and not run up on anyone and be careful not to shoot unless it's a deer or large game. We'll set several rabbit snares while we find a blind and watch for deer," replied Cobie.

"I'll make lunch for us if you'll pack the snares, extra ammo, and roll up our sleeping bags for the hunt," Cobie smiled at her daughter and pointed at the gear.

"We won't be out overnight so why bring the sleeping bags?"

"Because I said so and then there is the fact that we never have a clue what we will run into so we need to always be prepared for anything, my sweet little Mini-Me."

"Mom! I don't like that. I do like looking like you and hope to have big boobs like yours one day, but Mini Me sounds like I'm a dwarf Cobie," Cloe protested.

Cobie looked at her twelve-year-old daughter and prayed those men never found them. She would die trying to save her from those animals. She then wondered if the world would ever be safe again for twelve-year-old girls.

Bennie had gone off again, so Cobie and Cloe left the cabin after setting several traps around the front and back of their home. The cabin wasn't much, but it beat huddling outside in the rain. They always hid anything of value before leaving the cabin and kept their food hidden above the ceiling. They had found a small trap door in the bedroom closet that went up above the ceiling, and that became their hiding spot. Small actions such as the traps and hiding their valuables made the women feel a little safer even if the measures weren't a perfect solution to the dangers around them.

They slowly walked west through the forest as the sun rose slowly behind them. The leaves and twigs were still damp, so they made little noise as they hunted that morning to increase their larder. Cobie stopped several times to set rabbit snares along the paths worn into the brush and weeds. She showed her daughter how to rub her gloves in the soil to help hide the human scent. Then she attached the line with the noose to the top of a small sapling, and the trigger stick with its notch hooked into the notch she cut into another small tree. She fixed the noose, so it covered the animal trail, and the trap was set.

They set eight of the small game traps then wandered on west until they saw a large creek with a pool.

Cloe suggested, "That pool of water looks deep and inviting. When it gets warmer, we can bathe in it and swim."

"Boy, that sounds great. These sponge baths keep us from stinking but just barely. I would love to take a swim in it now if it were forty degrees warmer."

Cloe started to answer when her mom cautioned, "What was that sound? Hide behind that log."

They heard the sound of something shuffling through the brush and heard voices.

***

"Come on Joe, I was a member of the Polar Bear club back in my hometown north of Seattle. We would take a swim in Puget Sound every New Year's Day," Madison begged.

"Sorry, but it's too darned cold for me to stick my butt in that freezing water. You go ahead, and I'll stand watch for Polar Bears and Penguins while you freeze your butt off," Joe laughed as he resisted the temptation to jump into the six-foot-deep clear mountain water with the naked nymph.

Madison took her coat off, sat on a log and removed her shoes, and then started to remove her blouse and skirt, when Joe chimed in with, "Whoa, don't take your clothes off. You'll catch pneumonia."

Madison dropped her clothes, bra, and panties to the ground and then jumped into the water as Joe turned his head away.

"Madison, you'll freeze to death. Get out of the water please," he pleaded.

Even though she was freezing, Madison stayed in the water trying to tempt him to join her until he walked to the bank with a blanket where he begged her to come to him and get warm. She walked out of the water shivering as he wrapped his arms and the blanket around her naked body. She threw her arms around him and kissed him before he could turn his head.

He took her back to the cabin, and they made love on the couch. Joe thought *I could get used to having Madison around.*

***

Cloe whispered, "That woman was naked. They need to get a room."

Cobie was deep in thought since she remembered the handsome man from the encounter at the outfitter's store. She was jealous to see him in the arms of another woman and was ready to slink off into the woods when she heard a man speak.

"Stop doing that. Someone might see us out here."

"Joe, my husband is dead. Your girlfriend is dead. We are alone in the woods at the end of the world, and I just want us to be together and take care of each other," the woman blubbered as she sat in his lap with only the blanket around her as Cobie watched.

Cobie wished she could change places with the woman but knew her daughter came first, and they needed to head back to check their traps and get back to the cabin. The man picked the woman up in his arms and carried her away heading west. She guessed that meant that they lived close by and that scared her because she had felt they were alone in the woods.

The first trap hadn't been tripped, but the second and third had dead rabbits. Cobie showed Cloe how to take the animals from the snares and then reset them before moving to the next snares. All but the last one were empty, and it had a raccoon in it that was still alive and mad as hell. Every time they got close, it tried to bite them, so Cobie picked up a large rock and hurled it at the beast. She only hit it on the side and made it madder as it fought the snare, which only had trapped its hind leg. Cobie picked up another rock and this time she crushed its skull with the thrown missile.

"I was tired of Spam and potted meat; this will give us a welcome change for tonight's meal," Cobie jested.

"Well, at least we're not down to eating roadkill," Cloe responded with a chortle then asked, "Mom, do you think that couple are nice people?"

"I don't know for sure, but I think the man is one of the good ones. Did you notice how he looked away as the woman walked into the water naked and then when she came out again? The woman threw herself at the man, and he didn't take her up on ... err..."

"Sex, Mom, I know about sex. Perhaps the guy was gay, and women don't turn him on."

"Okay, I'm not having a talk about other people's mating habits with my twelve-year-old daughter. Let's get on to the cabin and clean these animals who gave up their lives to feed us," Cobie exclaimed.

"Well, how am I going to learn about mating habits if my Mom doesn't tell me? Besides, that nice man ran his hand under that blanket. What do you suppose he was doing?"

"It was none of our business what his hand was doing, but that's a fair question, and when you turn 16, we'll talk about mating habits. Until then zip your lips before I ground you for the rest of your life," an exasperated Cobie said.

"Not to push my luck, but what are you going to ground me from? We don't have TV, iPhones, shopping malls, or anything else fun."

"Smartass! I'll just beat you like they did in the old days when a child got uppity."

The next morning they decided to try their luck southeast of their cabin in hopes that the killers stuck to the roads to the northwest of their hunting camp. They wanted to travel about three miles southeast of the cabin to set up their camp for another two-day deer hunting trip. The terrain had more deep valleys and ridges to traverse, and their legs were worn out when they made camp late in the morning.

They ate a light lunch and headed another half mile east up a hill until they came to a gravel road that appeared to be well used.

"I thought we would avoid people by heading this way. We'll let's scout the area then head back down the hill to the valley and hunt there," Cobie told her daughter as they watched the road for several minutes before crossing.

Cobie and Cloe walked for another half mile when unexpectedly they were on the edge of an enormous clearing on the top of the mountainside. They walked south while staying in the cover of the forest until they saw a small ranch up ahead of them.

"Baby girl, stay here so I can scout the ranch. If anything happens head back to the cabin. Do not come to try to help me. I promise I will make it back and meet you back home."

"But Mom, I ..."

"Girl, trust me and do what I say. Now I'm going over to that house and check it out. If I'm not back in an hour, go fetch our stuff and get your tail back to the cabin. If I'm not home in two days, I won't be home. In that case, go find that couple we saw in the woods and try to get them to take you into their home. Make sure they know that you can hunt and fish and won't be a bother," Cobie said with a tight smile on her face.

"Mom, you are scaring me."

"Sorry, but as usual I want you prepared for anything. Now, hide until I come back."

Cobie went deeper into the woods and came out on the opposite side of the house to make sure anyone that saw her would think she came from that direction. She crept along the side of the barn and then a large storage shed before arriving about 25 feet from the house. She heard sounds coming from the back door. She crept closer, listened to a woman crying, and opened the kitchen door. She saw a naked woman hiding behind the kitchen table with a cut lip and blood flowing from

117

her nose. The woman had bruises all over her body and several cuts surrounded by dried blood.

Cobie moved toward her, but the woman waved frantically for Cobie to go away. Cobie grabbed a paper towel and began cleaning the women's face as she asked, "What happened? Who did this?"

"Get out of here before he comes back. He just went to the barn and will be back in a minute," the desperate woman pleaded.

"I won't go without you," Cobie answered.

The woman lifted her leg and showed Cobie the chain around her ankle that was bolted to the floor and urged, "Go, he will kill you, if you are lucky!"

Cobie heard a noise coming from the back porch and hid along the wall as she watched the man walk into the kitchen.

The man was older, had a large salt and pepper mustache, was dressed in camouflage print pants and shirt, and had a pistol in a holster on his belt. He sang a song that Cobie didn't know as he stood over the poor woman. Cobie patiently waited for the right opportunity when the man squatted down over the woman waving a pair of pliers in her face.

He said, "You will tell me what I want, and then I will mount you and leave you with child, Allah willing."

Cobie raised her rifle and butt stroked the man on the side of his head, and he fell to the floor dead. A large pool of blood formed around his head and the pungent odor of iron mixed with urine filled the room. Cobie choked back her desire to vomit and went on to help the captive lady.

Cobie was excited as she said, "The asshole is dead. I'll get the chain off you, and we can get the hell out of here."

Cobie searched the man's pockets, found the key to the lock, and took the chain off the woman's leg then said, "Grab a few clothes while I stuff my backpack with any food and let's get out of here to safety."

The woman stood on wobbly legs and left to her bedroom to fetch the clothes. Cobie found several cans of meat, vegetables, and tuna, which she added to her backpack. She tucked the man's 9mm Beretta into her waistband, and they left quickly heading to Cloe. They had only traveled a short way when there was a loud crack behind them, and the woman's head exploded. Blood, bone, and bits of brain matter splattered the side of Cobie's head. Before Cobie could turn around another crack of gunfire sounded. She felt a burning sensation on her right shoulder, and the bullet knocked her to the ground. Her shoulder throbbed and the pain was unbearable.

Cobie rolled over to see two men standing over her with pistols pointed at her.

"Bitch you killed my father. You will die and burn in hell for this sin against Allah. Abdula, shoot the cur dog."

The one called Abdul stood over Cobie and loosened his belt, "help me get her pants off. We might as well have some fun with this piece of crap."

The other one tried to unbuckle Cobie's belt, but she bit him on the arm as she tried to draw the Beretta from her belt. He grabbed her left hand and held it while taking the pistol.

He then slapped her, pulled her pants and panties down to her knees, and dropped down on her. There was a loud explosion, and the man fell off her, then another and the remaining thug fell to the ground. Cloe shot both men in the chest and ran to help dress her mom.

Cloe helped her mom pull her pants up then held her mom's head on her lap and asked, "Are you okay? We need to leave now in case someone heard the shots. I'll grab their pistols and then we need to get out of here."

"Baby girl, my arm hurts like hell."

Cloe examined the wounds and saw a small entry wound in the fleshy part of her shoulder that wasn't bleeding and a more extensive exit wound that was bleeding. She tore a hunk of cloth from her t-shirt, pushed the wadded cloth against her mom's exit wound, and tied it in place. She helped her mom to her feet, and they headed northeast to their camp as fast as her mom could walk.

They arrived at their camp, and Cloe checked the wound and then hid anything she couldn't carry. They plodded north instead of heading straight to the cabin so Cloe could try to throw any trackers off their trail. She found a rocky area to hide their tracks and doubled back to a tall ridge where she could watch for anyone following them. She then took care of her Mom's wound the best she could with the small first aid kit. She applied antibiotic salve and used gauze and surgical tape to bind the wound. She then lay prone on a rock with both deer rifles for the next several hours as she watched for anyone following them.

"Baby girl, if there were anyone following us we would have seen them. I can walk now so let's follow this rocky terrain for half a mile then head southwest to the cabin. I need to get home and rest."

"Mom, we should find a safe place and rest. The jarring keeps your wound bleeding. Please stop here and rest until morning. We are two and a half miles from that house, and there is no way anyone can track us across those rocks with the sun going down."

"Okay, you win, and I'm exhausted. Move over to that ledge over there and let's hide in those boulders where we can see anyone coming for 200 yards. I'll take turns on guard duty."

Cloe gave her mom several nonprescription painkillers and helped her into her sleeping bag. Even the rocky ground couldn't keep Cobie from falling asleep. Cloe fought sleep all night long but knew they might be killed in their sleep, so she walked around the area and stood the entire time to make sure she didn't fall asleep.

Cloe watched her mom sleep as the morning light crept its way over the mountains. The shadows were long, but there was enough light for them to travel, so she shook her mom until she woke up for the day.

"Thanks for taking my turn ... girl it's daylight. You must be dead on your feet."

Cloe yawned and then smiled, "I'm good to go. I'm not old like some people who need their beauty rest when they get a boo boo-ouwie."

Cobie laughed and pulled her daughter close with her good arm and hugged her for several minutes, "I love you, Cloe

Marie. We would make a great team even if you didn't obey me back at that ranch."

"Come on, Mom, let's hit the dusty trail."

***

The vehicle drove up to the ranch house, and no one greeted the leader of their cell, as he was accustomed, as was befitting of his rank in the organization. Perhaps, in the grand scheme of things, back home in Saudi Arabia, being the four-thousand one-hundred and seventy-third Prince of the House of Saud, might not be as important as he believed. Still, he was of the Royal Lineage of the House of Saud, and here, he was in charge.

"Omar, find Abdulla and make sure he understands that I am not to be kept waiting."

Omar took five men and headed into the house with one of the men to find Abdulla; he sent the others to find out what happened to the two that were supposed to be guarding the ranch and their prisoners.

Omar came out of the house and yelled, "Abdulla is dead."

The three men ran back to report Abdulla's two guards were also dead, and the captive was missing.

122

The leader said," "Find the ones responsible and bring them to me. Alive! We don't have time for this. We must leave for Portland by Friday."

☆

Chapter 10

Joe woke up with Madison in his arms, they were both naked and sharing the same sleeping bag. She had a slight Lilac smell coming from her hair that drove Joe crazy with desire. She felt fantastic in his arms, and he knew he would keep her there even if it were to use her as she had planned to use him. He was not ashamed of himself for giving into her charms and would think about that first night for many months to come. He thought if two people used each other to get what they wanted then no one is really harmed. Madison now knew exactly what Joe wanted from her, and he knew what she needed from him.

Joe started to get out of bed, but she felt too wonderful in his arms. He stroked her hair and then ran the back of his fingers across her face. Her skin was soft and inviting, so he began making love to her slowly and gently. Madison woke, rolled on top of Joe, and pinned him down with kisses. She then took charge, which shocked Joe at first then drove him crazy for the next hour. When Madison was through, they both lay on top of the sleeping bag exhausted, and she quickly fell back to sleep.

He slid out of bed without waking her and had the fire going in a few minutes. It was still dark outside, and the fire had burned down to a few red coals. He wanted to warm the cabin up a bit for Madison's comfort. It would be out before daybreak, and he was not worried about someone spotting the smoke.

He was pissed at himself for agreeing to make a scavenging run into Ashland during a weak moment last night. That woman was an expert at manipulating men and Joe thought she was good at many other things also. He couldn't stay mad at her anymore but knew he needed to keep her from pushing him into anything dangerous.

Joe cut some dried strips of venison into a pot full of yesterday's soup and let the concoction heat while he shaved and performed his morning bathroom rituals. When finished he went back to the bedroom and woke Madison by gently stroking her face.

"Good morning sunshine," Joe whispered in her ear.

"I don't see any sun. Come on back to bed so we can take up where we left off. Our trip can wait a day," she pleaded.

"It is 1:30 and it will be a beautiful morning with a high of 45 degrees in sunny downtown forest in the mountains. Wake up sleepy head. You are the one who talked me into making another run into town. We have to scavenge, find what we need, and then be back here before daybreak," urged Joe to a sleepy Madison.

"Oh, yes. Make sure you have that list I put together for you last night. I really need those feminine hygiene products and makeup. Don't forget the spices. We need to spice up the taste of our food. Pardon the pun," Madison nagged.

Joe remembered the list and that he would need a semi-truck to haul all of the items on the list back to the cabin.

"I won't forget, but you have to get your butt in gear if you're going to be my pack mule," Joe joked about their deal that he would go into town while she waited at the golf course to help him bring the supplies back to the cabin.

Madison kissed Joe on the neck and said, "Funny you didn't think I was a pack mule when we were sharing my sleeping bag last night and again this morning," she joked.

Madison put on a pair of Joe's pants and had to use a rope to cinch up the slack around her waist. She wore a hat over her ponytail and amazingly was ready in ten minutes, which astounded Joe.

Joe smiled broadly at Madison's tightly cinched pants and said, "I think we both need some new pants, mine are getting a bit too big even for me."

In the short time, since Joe began his new life, the work, and exercise he got just from surviving had cut significantly into his girth.

They only took Joe's rifle and a 9mm pistol for each of them, and empty backpacks along with two duffel bags to haul their booty back to the cabin. Joe added two bottles of water for each of them, and they headed out the door for their five and a half mile hike down to Ashland.

He planned to leave Madison at the Oak Knoll Golf Club then sneak in and out of town before daylight. He would avoid Walmart, Target, and other significant chain stores because they were probably picked clean. He hoped he would find what they needed at restaurants, gas stations, and the golf course clubhouse.

The trip down the mountain was almost as brutal as the trip back would be because their calves screamed at them after a few miles of continually walking downhill. Joe chose to head to town going straight down the mountain to shorten the trip and to avoid encountering anyone on the road. He decided not to drive the Jeep because it could be heard for miles on the gravel roads and the big lugs on the tires made a distinctive whine on the pavement. This had to be a stealth mission.

Madison had a great body that looked like she was in shape but had no stamina at all. She huffed and puffed after a mile and mentioned several times that her calves hurt. They had to stop four times on the way down, and Joe knew they would need those forty minutes of darkness on the way home.

"Come on girl, we have to plod on, or we might as well turn back now," Joe preached.

"I'm sorry that I'm not in as good shape as you are. Mr. Mountain man, I'm doing the best I can. Let's go," an exhausted Madison said in a strained voice.

They finally arrived at the clubhouse without seeing anyone and only a few plumes of smoke coming from chimneys along the way. Joe wondered if the area might be safer than he had thought if people were broadcasting their existence. Joe searched the clubhouse for any people or other dangers; he found none and left Madison to search for items on their list. She ran over to him and gave him a good luck kiss. He waved goodbye, and he was quickly on his way.

Joe walked across the fairways headed west and was very quiet as he walked through a small subdivision beside Highway 5. There were no lights on in the houses, and many of them had burned to the ground. Several had bullet holes and broken glass from fierce fighting. He saw cars that looked as though someone had emptied a machine gun into them. He left the neighborhood and stayed in the shadows as he progressed to his first target, which was a Mexican restaurant. He had eaten there several times while waiting for the lawyers and signing paperwork before the shit hit the fan.

The doors to the restaurant were shattered, and all the windows were broken, but the place had not burned. Joe cautiously entered with his 9mm drawn and ready for a fight. The cash registers were open and lay on the floor. Why anyone needed money, these days escaped Joe as he plodded on through the building to the kitchen. The place was bare of any food, but there were plenty of jars and bottles of spices. He filled his backpack until it was full and was tickled to have found two unopened bottles of Sriracha sauce.

He then went to the pantry and found it empty, so he found the broom closet and hit pay dirt. There were cartons of toilet paper, feminine hygiene products, and hand soap. He filled his tote bag to the brim and headed back to the clubhouse to drop his treasure and make another run into town for food. He heard a sound in the dining room and fell to the floor.

He couldn't figure out what the noise sounded like but he was confident someone had followed him into the restaurant, and he knew there would be a fight. He decided to confront whoever was making the sound and perhaps scare them away without anyone dying this night.

"I've got a gun. Leave, and I won't have to shoot you," Joe yelled.

He heard a sound behind him that scared him and turned to see a dog lying at his feet.

"Rover you scared the crap out of me. Boy, you look skinny. You need to learn how to hunt rabbits," he said as he noticed the rope trailing behind the poor animal.

Joe cut the rope and got back to his search for supplies. He didn't find anything of interest, so he headed out the back door toward the golf course. He didn't see anyone out, but a few dogs barked in the distance, and there was gunfire north of him as he walked back to the clubhouse. Madison wasn't in sight, but there were several piles of household supplies, hygiene products and several bottles of whiskey in her collections. He heard a sound behind him and turned to see Madison hauling more supplies to the room.

"I'm going to a doctor's office just across Highway 5 and another restaurant, and I should be back before 4 am. That will still give us plenty of darkness, and we will head home with what we can carry. Hide what you want to save for another trip. This dog followed me back from the restaurant, he'll keep you company. I'll be right back," Joe said to Madison as he left the room.

She said, "Be careful Joe. I'm starting to like you."

Joe walked across Highway 5 in front of the Mexican restaurant and headed to the doctor's office he had seen while shopping in Ashland. The office windows were shattered; the glass doors had been rammed by a log that still lay in the doorway. Joe entered the building with his gun drawn to see a mess of office furniture and computers strewn around on the floor. He went into the exam rooms and found they had also been tossed by someone who probably wanted drugs and not medical supplies. He found bandages, antibiotics, and a plethora of medical supplies that had been thrown on the floor by the looters.

He opened the door to the Doctor's office, and a rotten smell of death poured out of the room. A quick glance showed the doctor lying on the floor with his head bashed in and a pool of dried blood around him. Joe closed the door and left the building with his bag full and a sincere desire to wipe that memory from his mind.

The next restaurant was a steakhouse, and again he only found spices and hygiene products; however, he did find a Glock 17 and a box of bullets in the manager's desk.

With his bags full, he headed back to the clubhouse to collect Madison and their booty so they could make the long hike back up the mountain. It was four o'clock, and they had an hour and a half to be in the woods and on their way to safety before it started getting light outside. Joe walked quickly across Highway 5 and past the restaurant on his way back to the golf course thinking the mission had at least gotten

Madison off his back and would improve the taste of their food.

Joe felt the hair on the back of his neck stiffen as he entered the front door to the clubhouse but couldn't put his finger on what bothered him. He slowly turned around and saw the issue. There were tire tracks on the outdoor carpet in front of the main entrance. They weren't there before. He looked around and saw the hat he'd given Madison to wear that day. He looked about outside, and then he entered the clubhouse to search for her. The supplies had been sorted, and she had selected the items to go with them but had not hidden the rest as discussed. She was nowhere to be found as he searched each room.

He went down the stairs to the locker rooms and entered the lady's locker room. He shined his flashlight around and saw the dog dead on the floor with a bullet wound in its side. The fact that Madison had been killed or kidnapped didn't hit Joe until he saw the dead dog. He flew into a rage and beat his hand on the mirror on the door breaking the mirror and cutting his hand in three places.

He sat down on a bench and sobbed for the first time in many years. Losing his best friend, his Grandma dying, the end of the world, and now losing the only friend he had walloped him in the gut, as nothing had ever hurt him before. He was mad at the people who took her as well as himself for not knowing what to do to save her or for that matter where to start. He didn't love Madison but she was one more thing life had taken from him, and it was the last straw.

He drew his gun and looked at it while contemplating the impossible when he heard a voice in his mind.

Dear Joe:

Grow a pair of balls and yank yourself up by the bootstraps. Don't let them win. Make a plan, go get Madison, and kill those fuckers.

Love Grandma.

That startled Joe back into reality, and he shook his head to clear his thoughts and holstered his 9mm. He thought about all those letters from Grandma that were left to read, gathered his loot, and headed back to the cabin to plan his next move. He knew there was no way he could stick around and search for Madison in Ashland, and his best guess was that the people who took her weren't still in the city. He thought about how to find her without being killed the entire time he walked up the mountain.

He was back at the old cabin before he realized he had walked so far without stopping. During the walk, he decided to move back to his other cabin and dropped all his bags there on the way. The only thing that kept popping into his mind was finding the young woman and her daughter and warning them about the danger. His other thought on finding the kidnappers was that these men had a vehicle and weren't afraid to drive around. He could stake out the intersection of Highways 5 and 66, and eventually, they would cross paths.

He thought he should find the women first to keep them from becoming victims. While he cooked his supper, he thought about where to begin his search for the women and figured that he should start at the pool in the creek and head east.

Joe woke up and immediately thought about that voice in his head, so he picked up the book of letters and thumbed his way to the back to look up suicide. The list was two pages long, and he was glad that Grandma had not thought a letter on suicide was necessary, so he tried pain and suffering. He saw the loss of a loved one and found the referenced message.

Dear Joe:

It's now a year since you started reading my letters. You lost your best friend and me, and I hope you have recovered. I hope you have a new love interest in your life to care for you and to discuss things with you. One should never intentionally try to be alone. We are social animals and need other people. Shake off losses and work hard to move on in life but never forget the ones you love. I could say crap like "don't cry over spilt milk," but that doesn't make the pain of the loss go away. I can say that you have to man up and do what it takes to survive and prosper in this mean old world. Don't be a victim.

Love Grandma.

His sleep was fitful at best that night as he second-guessed leaving Madison alone at the clubhouse and his not being able to follow the kidnappers. Grandma's letter helped assuage the pain, and he did feel stronger after reading the letter. He thought about the letters and wanted to be as good a person as his grandma had been and still was thanks to the letters.

He ate cold rabbit stew from the night before and readied his backpack for a three-day excursion to the east section of his property. The eastern half was the only part he had not explored thoroughly. He felt the women might be on his property, but the kidnappers had to have a place on one of the improved roads to the northeast of his property.

Joe struck out for the creek and quickly found the old tracks, which he followed north until he lost them, high on the ridge north of the stream. He stopped and pondered for a while and felt the women's northerly trek had been an effort to lead people away from their camp. He then walked east only a few feet into the woods at the top of the ridge to pick up their tracks. The forests were overgrown with sticker bushes, vines, and small saplings making travel rough. He found a few fast food wrappers, coke cans, and soggy newspapers but no signs of the women.

He never found their tracks, but he did see the black Jeep that had sped out of town ahead of him on the day TSHTF. He knew they would have to be close by and slowly headed down the hillside barely able to keep his footing. He was in a controlled slide down the slope when his progress was stopped by an old pile of wood. He looked around and was surprised to see a small cabin in the woods ahead of him. He waited for fifteen minutes before moving closer. Then Bennie greeted him with a wagging tail and began licking Joe's face.

"Hey, Bennie. This must be where the women are staying. Take me to your mistress."

Joe followed Bennie up to the cabin from the rear, looked in the window, and saw the cabin was dark on the inside. He shined his flashlight onto the window and found himself staring into a bedroom with a woman asleep in the bed. He turned the flashlight off and turned to see a girl with a rifle pointed at his chest.

134

"Drop your guns asshole. I said drop them, or you're going to have a big hole in your chest," the young girl said forcefully.

Joe lowered his rifle to the ground and said, "I can explain. I'm ..."

The girl interrupted, "A dead man if you don't drop that pistol. Do it now, or I shoot. Don't try anything because I have the trigger pulled on this 30.30 and I'm holding the hammer back with my thumb. I'm getting tired, and you're about to die."

Joe pulled the pistol from its holster with two fingers and laid it on the ground along with the rifle. He still had a Glock in his waistband and decided not to tell the girl about it unless forced to do so. He raised his hands and asked, "Why are you holding the gun on me. You are trespassing on my land and squatting in my cabin. I'm Joe Harp, and I own this entire hillside and the land for a half a mile in all directions. Please, put your gun down."

The girl released the trigger and leaned the rifle against the cabin as she drew a Beretta and kept Joe covered, "Turn around and walk up on the porch. Now plop your ass down with your back to the wall and take your boots off."

The girl had removed her shoestrings and ordered Joe to tie his right wrist to his lower leg. She visually checked the job before she picked up his pistol and stuck it in her belt.

Joe replied, "I'm not going to harm you. Wake your mom up and let me talk to her."

Bennie sat down beside Joe and tried to lick his face when the girl admonished him and pulled him away by his collar.

"Bennie, get away from him. He's a terrorist," the girl said.

"Look I just came to ..."

"Shut up and speak when spoken to asshole. Why did you come to our cabin?"

"I already told you it's my cabin. I came here to warn you about some people who kidnapped a friend of mine. You two women are alone up here and could be the kidnappers next victims," Joe stated.

The girl poked Joe in the ribs with the Beretta, "You are probably the kidnapper or working for those bastards. I should shoot you like I did the ones who shot my mom."

"Whoa, girl. Has your mom been shot?"

"Yes, but you aren't going to get close to her. I'll kill you before you get close to her like those terrorists did," Cloe said.

"Cloe, who is the man," a voice behind Joe said in a weak voice.

The girl jumped to her feet and said, "Mom, be careful. This man could be one of those men from back at the ranch."

Joe awkwardly raised his head, and Cobie instantly recognized him from Cobb's Outfitter's store and said, "You're the young man who inherited a bunch of money and land around Ashland. I saw you at Cobbs."

"Your daughter isn't impressed by my inheritance, and I'm sorry to say money is worthless now; however, I do own this cabin and the land around it," Joe smiled as he spoke.

"Cloe, please untie Mr. Harp's hands and give his shoes back to him. He won't hurt us," Cobie said as she stumbled back into the cabin.

Cloe charged in behind her mom and found her half on the couch where she had fallen. Cobie looked up and said, "Cloe untie the man, and then you can tend to me."

Cloe untied Joe's hand and gave him his pistol back. Joe entered the cabin and saw Cobie lying on the couch.

"Where were you shot? Let me see your wound," Joe queried.

Cobie rolled to her side, and Joe peeled off the bandages to show an angry red wound that desperately needed attention. Joe opened his backpack, cleaned the wounds, squeezed antibiotic salve on both injuries, and said, "Ladies, I'm going back to my cabin and fetch some antibiotic pills. You need to fight this infection from the inside also."

Cloe cried as she said, "Will mom be okay? Please go get the pills."

"She will be fine a few days after we get these pills into her. I'll be back in about two hours with the pills," Joe answered.

Joe left his backpack and took the same route back to his cabin even though going in a straight line would have saved an hour because he was still worried about these men stumbling upon them. He arrived at the cabin and placed the medical items he needed in his pockets and added enough food for all of them for several days before heading back.

Joe was about halfway there as he walked in the edge of the woods when a strange looking vehicle drove slowly by his position and stopped. Joe froze as he watched the vehicle with the machine gun mounted on top disgorge four men who walked around the intersection where a dirt road headed north off this main gravel road.

The men spoke in a foreign language, and the only thing Joe understood was Allahu Akbar. The men piled back in the vehicle and headed east toward town. The driver and passenger were scanning the ground as though they were looking for tracks. The car was out of sight when Joe decided to head deeper into the woods and angle down to the cabin to make sure he couldn't be seen from the woods.

Joe thought, *"Holy crap. These are Islamic Terrorists here in the mountains of Oregon."*

***

Cloe saw Joe's backpack lying by the door and rifled through it to see if she could learn anything about this man. She found survival gear, some food, and two small envelopes. She took them to her mom and said, "Mom he had these envelopes in his backpack. Let's read them and find out if he is a terrorist, or maybe a crook."

"Cloe, usually I'd be upset with you for looking through a stranger's gear but hand those envelopes to me."

The envelopes weren't sealed, so Cobie opened one and saw:

Dear Joe:

It's now a year since you started reading my letters. You recently lost your girlfriend and me, and I hope you have recovered. I hope you have a new love interest in your life to care for you and to discuss things with. One should never intentionally try to be alone. We are social animals and need other people. Shake off losses and work hard to move on in life but never forget the ones you love. I could say crap like "don't cry over spilt milk," but that doesn't make the pain of the loss go away. I can say that you have to man up and do what it takes to survive and prosper in this mean old world. Don't be a victim.

Love Grandma.

The short letter had tears and a couple of smudges on it, so she knew their visitor had already read the sweet letter from his Grandmother. The note made Joe look like a great guy, and stirred Cobie's interest to find out more about the man who was helping them, so she opened the next letter.

Dear Joe:

Almost four weeks should have passed since you started reading my daily letters from the grave. You should have found all three cabins, the large creek, and the deep pool. Your Grandpa and I used to have picnics by the stream and went skinny dipping in that pool when we were much younger. We loved that property and enjoyed it for over 60 years. Please don't ever sell it or let anyone build condominiums on it. That would spoil it forever. Remember money isn't worth spit in the end, but love lasts forever. I hope you find your one true love and you two enjoy the property for another 30 years like Grandpa, and I did. I know it's a bit early for you to be thinking about women yet because of how Gwen treated you but don't give up on love. Love and companionship are two of the most important things in this world, and true love can't be purchased.

Well, I ramble on and am getting a bit tired. This disease is kicking this old girl's butt, and I need a nap. Goodbye until the next letter.

Love Grandma.

Cobie had tears flowing as she read the letter and felt the pain this young man must be suffering from the loss of his beloved Grandmother and some kind of problem with a woman. Cobie placed the letter back in its envelope and had Cloe, put it back in his backpack.

"Mom, you were crying. What was in the letter that caused you to cry?"

"Baby girl, I shouldn't have read the letter. This man has suffered several losses and is trying to find himself. He just inherited a huge tract of land when his Grandmother died and has had other personal problems. Be gentle with him. Please."

"Mom, that letter doesn't prove that he isn't a pervert. Those Senators and Hollywood types were well thought of in their communities, and they still were pedophiles and attacked women and children several years ago," insisted Cloe.

"Cloe, give it a break. You have a pistol and me to watch over you, so I don't think he will attack you," her mom said.

***

As he walked to the women's cabin, he wondered why any self-respecting terrorist would be stuck in Ashland Oregon where there are no important targets. The entire situation didn't make sense, but he knew the tires on that vehicle made the tracks back at the golf course, and these men had Madison. He would find them and kill every one of the bastards. He prayed Madison was still alive.

He arrived at the cabin and shouted to make sure little Annie Oakley didn't drill him when he walked into the cabin. Cobie was on the couch with a pillow behind her head, and the young girl was making her drink some water.

Joe opened the bottle and offered Cobie two of the pills, which she washed down with the water and said, "Sorry about my manners, this is Cloe, and I'm Cobie Simms. I saw you at Cobbs, and I believe you walked up when that man and I were in a heated discussion."

Joe took his hat off and replied, "I'm Joe Harp, and I remember you from that day. I remember thinking that you were beautiful and mad as hell at that man."

Joe immediately blushed when he realized he had told her that he thought she was beautiful. He gazed at her laying there and couldn't break contact with her alluring eyes. He smiled and listened to her response.

"Well, thanks for the compliment. Now down to business, will you be evicting us from your land? I'm sorry about squatting here, but we were unfairly evicted from our apartment and had to quickly find a place to stay until we found something," the beautiful black haired lady said with tears streaming down her eyes.

"No, you can stay here as long as you want. I have a nice snug cabin and don't need this one," Joe smiled at Cobie.

"I'll bet its snug with that blonde snuggled up against you like back at the creek," Cloe exclaimed.

Joe stared at the young girl and said, "That blonde was only a friend needing help, and she was kidnapped by the same people that are looking for you two. I saw one of their vehicles up on the road on top of the ridge, and the same vehicle left tracks where Madison was kidnapped. We were in town scavenging for supplies, and they found her while I was gathering things we needed. Oh, and it's not nice to spy on people."

Cobie said, "We need so many things, but I was afraid to go into town. I got shot trying to help a woman escape this gang and my daughter had to rescue me when they killed the woman and shot me."

Joe replied, "I'm going to carry you to bed so you can get rested and I will stay with you two until you get your strength back. It's the least I can do for two cowgirls stranded by the apocalypse."

Cloe replied, "We don't need ..." when her mom interrupted and said, "We do need your help, and you can sleep on the couch. We don't have much, but Cloe is a good cook."

Joe laughed and replied, "You concentrate on getting better. Cloe and I will call a truce and try to get along. I brought some food and other supplies from my home to keep me from being a burden. Cloe, please unpack that green bag and find something to fix for supper. Please."

Joe picked the small woman up in his arms and started to the bedroom when suddenly there was a squeal from behind him. Joe turned with the raven-haired beauty to see Cloe beaming with delight.

"Mom he brought toilet paper, soap, tampons, and candy bars," Cloe was delighted.

Cobie's very red face was only inches away from Joe's face when she replied, "My daughter has struggled with the leaves and catalog paper. You are her new hero."

Joe replied in his best cowboy voice, "Mam, I'm just a simple cowboy trying to bring comfort and joy to two cowgirls in need of help. I gathered those supplies the other day, and I think you can use them more than I can."

"Boy, that sounded fake. You need to work on the cowboy accent," Cobie chuckled.

Joe placed Cobie on the bed and covered her with a blanket before leaving to join her daughter in the kitchen. Cobie watched them make peace for a few minutes and fell fast asleep. She felt safe for the first time in many weeks, and perhaps this old cabin wasn't the worst thing that could have happened to them.

Joe sat by the fireplace that night after Cloe had gone to bed and pulled the two letters from his Grandma out of his pack. He read the second letter and laughed when he read the words about women and not giving up on love. Joe started to put the letters away when he noticed a smudge in the ink. He brought the letter closer to the fire and could see where drops of water had been on the letter. He examined the envelope and didn't find any water stains. This made him search his pack, and he was confident someone had searched through his belongings.

He was furious at first but then calmed down and tried to put himself in their place. Two women all alone with a stranger in their midst would be suspicious and want to know more about the man. Then he blushed because he remembered what they saw in the letter.

☆

Chapter 11

Cloe was up early and closed the door to the bedroom before she began rattling the pots and pans in the kitchen. She started a fire in the cook stove and then made sure Joe was up for the day by sending him outside to fetch some water. She cut up a freshly caught rabbit, added canned potatoes, and carrots to the pan and set it on the old wood-fired cook stove. Joe marveled at how industrious the young girl was for this early in the morning and did his best to help her get their meal prepared.

Cloe finished cooking the stew while Joe brought wood into the kitchen and another load for the fireplace. Since it was still dark outside, he threw an armload on the fire and heated the now cold cabin to nice toasty warmth.

"My mom says not to have a fire in the daytime because someone might see the smoke," Cloe informed Joe, and then added, "it's also a waste of wood, and we don't have a lot of wood."

"Your mom is right about the smoke, but you got up super early, and we still have about two hours before daylight, and with these tall trees around the cabin, no one could see the smoke anyway. I'll go get some wood after we eat and build up a good supply before I leave you two charming ladies to yourselves," Joe replied.

Cloe tried to think of a smart assed reply but was genuinely grateful for the help with the wood and the medicine for her mom. Cloe told Joe to be seated and served him a generous portion of the stew.

"Cloe, do you ever miss breakfast cereal or Pop Tarts? Boy, I sure do. I'm a bachelor and grabbed food on the run before TSHTF."

Cloe said, "I miss pancakes the most and then ice cream. We always had bacon, eggs, orange juice, and pancakes for breakfast on Sundays before going to church. I miss church too."

Joe thought back to the days when his mom woke him up early on Sunday mornings and told him to get his butt in gear for Sunday school. She always prepared ham and eggs, toast with blackberry jam, and orange juice every Sunday morning. He and his dad were always moving slowly, but his mom still got them to church on time. Now he felt guilty about not going to church with her as often as he should have, and now he didn't know if his mom and dad were even still alive. Tears came to his eyes, and he quickly wiped them away while Cloe looked the other way to reach the pepper.

Joe finished a mouthful of the rabbit stew and said, "My, your mom was right this is great stew. How did you learn to cook like this?"

Cloe smiled back at Joe and replied, "My mom taught me how to cook, and she is a better cook than me."

Joe looked back to the bedroom and said, "Go check on your mom and see if the fever has gone down. Give her two more of the antibiotic pills."

"Please," Cloe said.

"Please, what?" Joe answered.

"Asshole, I'm not your daughter or your slave so say please, and we will get along much better," said Cloe.

"You are a feisty young lady. Please go help your mom."

"That's better. We will continue to work on your manners and perhaps I won't have to call you an asshole so much."

A voice rang out from the back of the cabin, "Cloe Marie, watch your mouth and don't call Mr. Harp names. At least try to act like an adult. He is here helping us."

Joe laughed and stuck his tongue out at the girl who promptly gave him a middle finger as she left the room. Joe broke out laughing and slapped his hand on the table.

"Cobie, I'm going outside to fetch some firewood. I'll also run your rabbit traps while I'm out," said Joe.

Cobie replied, "Please let Cloe go with you when you run the traps. We need to learn how to improve our traps. There are thousands of rabbits out there, and we aren't catching that many."

"I'd love to take her with me and teach her what I know after I get the wood cut and stacked," Joe responded and went outside into the cold, early spring air.

"Mom, I don't like that man, and I'll bet he abuses young girls like me."

"Cloe, I think he is a good man and wouldn't hurt anyone who doesn't hurt him first. I like that you are protective of me, but I'm a grown woman and have had more experience around men. This one is a good one, and I don't want you to run him off."

Cloe thought for a minute and said, "You don't like him, do you? He's fat and ugly and not too bright."

"I think he is very handsome and intelligent for a man. You know none of them are too bright, but we have to put up with them," her mom joked.

Cloe didn't like her mom's answer, "Do you want him to move in with us and be your boyfriend?

"No, it's too early for that kind of thinking, but I would like to get to know him better before I have thoughts like that. I do know that having him around will help us find more food and make us safer. Don't antagonize him," Cloe's mom warned.

Cloe wouldn't let it die and said, "So are you going to go skinny dipping with him in the pool just to keep him around?"

"Cloe that was a terrible thing to say about me. I'm not going to lead him on just to keep him around. I'm very disappointed in you for your behavior. Treat Joe nicely as long as he treats us nicely. Stop causing trouble when there is none to be found. Now go outside and help Joe stack the firewood. Let me know before you two go running the traps," her mom ordered.

Joe had gathered large limbs from the forest floor and used a handsaw to cut them to a useable length. He had cut several arms full of wood and Cloe helped him bring the wood into the cabin.

Cobie felt a bit stronger and moved to the couch after she dressed. Her shoulder hurt like hell and was still in a sling. She greeted them as they brought the first armful into the cabin. Cloe went back for another load when Cobie grabbed Joe's hand, "My you two make a great team and haven't killed each other yet this morning."

"Yeah, well, the day ain't over yet, but yes, you have a great young woman there."

"Joe, I haven't dated in years, so Cloe is very protective of me and hasn't been around men very much. We spend most of our time together when I'm not working or going to school, so she is jealous of my time. Please bear with her and things will get better," Cobie said.

Joe replied, "Cloe is great and not a problem for me. Actually, I like her because she is so feisty and protective of you. I don't need to remind you that women will have it much tougher than men in this new screwed up world and will have to be tougher than in the past."

"Joe, I agree with what you said, but I think you are a good man and she needs to cut you some slack. I'd be lying if I said I don't want you to stay because that's not true. You can help hunt food and help keep us safe, but I won't lead you on and flirt with you to keep you around," Cobie said as her face turned red.

Joe smiled and said, "Thanks for being honest. That blonde Cloe saw was just the opposite. She threw herself at me so I would take care of her. She started working hard to help, but I could see she was just trying to fool me until she had her hooks into me. I wanted her to go away, but not be kidnapped. I think those men have her and I plan to kill them when I get a chance. I hate to say it, but I think it's too late for Madison."

"Did she?' Cobie asked.

"Excuse me. Did Madison what?"

Cobie frowned and asked, "Did she get her hooks into you?"

"She tried," was all he said.

The answer didn't help, and Cobie wanted to know more about this young man. She found herself very jealous of Madison and mad at Joe for being with the woman. She suddenly remembered the men talking on the walkie-talkies the other day and said, "Joe, do you drive a Bronco?"

"Yes, why do you ask?"

"The other day we were listening to our walkie-talkies and heard two men talking about hurting a man driving a Bronco up Indian Head road. They didn't say why."

"That has to be me. I guess they just want my Bronco."

She reached for Joe's hand and said, "Please be careful."

"Don't worry, I'll be safe. Cloe and I are going to head out to run the traps this morning, and I'll work on building up the meat supply. I'll need to hunt for deer before that venison that I brought over, runs out, and as much as I hate it, I'll have to make a scavenging run back into town to try to find some vegetables. Cloe needs the vitamins and stuff you get from eating veggies. I'll also look for vitamin supplements to help us until I can grow a garden. If you help tend the garden I'll share the bounty," Joe said.

Cloe walked into the room, and Cobie replied, "And you can beat her with a log if she gets out of control."

Cloe replied, "Mom, don't give this guy any ideas. If he tries to spank me with a log, I'll shoot him."

"Cloe!"

"I think she would. So I'll pass on the log, but Cloe let's make sure you understand when we walk out that door you will do what I say when I say, and I'll bring you back safe. If you can't agree to that then you can go by yourself or stay home and let me tend to the traps," Joe said in a firm voice.

Cloe was thinking about what Joe said when her mom replied, "Cloe will stay here since she is having trouble agreeing to your terms."

"Mom, I agree, and yes ma'am; I'll do what Joe says."

'Well tell him."

"Joe I'll do what you say as long as you keep your hands to yourself," the young girl said.

Her mom was about to lay into her when Joe spoke, "Why would any man want to mess with a skinny loud-mouthed brat like you. I can find full-grown women in the woods all over the place around here that won't talk back and are much better company," Joe laughed then added, "Your honor will be safe in my presence. Now squirt, get your gear, and get your butt in motion so we can leave."

Cloe went into the bedroom, and Cobie said with a straight face, "Don't bring any of those full-grown women back here to this cabin Mr. Harp," before laughing.

Joe ignored the implied meaning and said, "You have a strong-willed young girl who will become a great woman in a few years, and you will have to keep a close eye on her,"

"Bring her back safe."

"I will. I promise," Joe said as they gazed into each other's eyes for a second when he broke away to look down at the floor.

Cobie felt terrible about keeping most of their food hidden in the place above the ceiling. She trusted this new man in her life, but her first responsibility was to Cloe and would always put her before anyone else.

They had to leave Bennie in the cabin with Cobie to prevent the noisy dog from following them into the woods.

They only walked a short way before Joe began Cloe's lessons on hunting and trapping.

"We need to make as little noise as possible as we walk through the forest because we might walk up on a deer or other game animal. We will mostly hunt at sunup because the deer begin moving at that time. Now see the rabbit trap that you set. It looks great, but the snare had sprung and didn't catch a rabbit. We can improve it by poking sticks in the ground around the backside and up the sides. This funnels the game to the bait and the snare. They have to stand on top of the snare to eat the leaves," Joe explained.

"That makes sense. Mom and I should have thought about doing that," Cloe said in frustration.

"Cloe, my dad taught me how to trap, and his dad taught him how to trap. You and your mom have done better than most people have. I will help you do better. My dad and I never trapped big game, so there is a lot for me to learn also." Joe said.

They walked on for an hour walking from trap to trap with Joe teaching her the tricks of how to trap. She was becoming more comfortable around him, and he noticed her words became softer as the day wore on. He found it easy to work with her the less combative she became and shared every bit of the trapping and hunting tips he knew.

"Look, Cloe, those tracks by the stream are from raccoons, and those are from a deer. The raccoons like to wash everything they eat, and the deer just stopped for a drink. This would be a great spot to build a deer blind. We could get some nice venison for steaks and stew."

Cloe looked to her right and said, "Look, those are people tracks."

Joe's heart skipped a beat as he joined her to look at the tracks. He saw two sets of tracks. One track was smaller than the other was and had a distinctive pattern. Joe made a print with his boot and asked Cloe to tell him what she could about the three footprints in the dirt.

"Well, yours is the largest, that one is smaller, and the third is the smallest. I think the other tracks are from two kids. One is bigger than the other," Cloe said.

"Please make a footprint next to that one," Joe said as he pointed at one of the smallest footprints.

Cloe did as he asked and saw that the prints were the same. "Joe, I made that print. Wow, I can now track me, and where I've been."

"So, whose is the other track?"

"It has to be mom's footprint."

"Cloe, what I'm about to tell you is very important and more critical for your survival. If we can track these prints, so can the men looking for you and your mom. Go over in the bushes and cut a small branch to use to sweep away those tracks."

She swept away the tracks, and they finished running the traps. They had three rabbits from the dozen traps, but more importantly, Cloe now knew how to improve her traps. She and her mom would catch more rabbits thanks to Joe. He also gave her training on how to leave as few footprints as possible on the way home. He even taught her to avoid walking to and from the cabin the same way to avoid wearing a trail into the ground.

Joe knocked on the door before entering the cabin so he wouldn't scare Cobie. She had lunch prepared and moved around the cabin much better even with her arm in the sling. She was still in pain but felt much better.

"The snares caught three rabbits, and Cloe is out back skinning them. I taught her how to make a few changes that will increase the number of rabbits she catches. We also saw your tracks on the bank of a stream about half a mile from here. I trained her how to sweep away the footprints and how to reduce the tracks you leave while walking through a forest," he said.

"How did my little bullheaded munchkin do today?"

"She is a great young lady. I think she is getting used to me because she didn't growl as much as the day went on. I'm hungry. What's for lunch?"

Cobie replied, "I'm afraid it is rabbit stew. We don't have much variety, and I'm almost out of spices so it will soon be bland stew."

"I think I can help with the spices. I found a bunch of them during my scavenger hunt in Ashland and brought them back to my cabin," he replied.

"That would be great. Wait, it's not just salt and pepper is it?"

"I know I don't look like a cook, but I do use spices and several different ones. I have chili powder, Cayenne, Oregano,

155

Cilantro, Allspice, Thyme, and Turmeric. And a big can of salt," Joe proudly said.

"Well, well, you do have some good spices there. Will you share if we cook," Cobie asked?

"I will fetch them from my cabin tomorrow. I will also bring some venison back to add to our larder."

Cloe came bouncing in after cleaning the rabbits and frowned when she saw her mom and Joe smiling at each other as they talked.

"Mom, I'm starving. What's for lunch?"

"We are lucky today. We are dining on pork chops, green beans, corn, and a garden salad," Cobie said followed by a big laugh.

"Rabbit stew again. Yummy. I just love rabbit stew," Cloe joked as she sat down at the table.

"I'm going to lay in some more wood for you girls today. Tomorrow I will travel to my cabin and bring some supplies and spices back to share with you. Later, when spring comes, I'll share some seeds for a garden. I plan to build a hothouse to start seeds before the weather breaks so I can get a head start on my garden," Joe informed the two.

"Cloe would be happy to go with you to help carry the supplies back here. Wouldn't you dear?"

"Mom, we barely know the man and yet you are sending your only daughter out with a man who could be a child molester," the girl replied.

Joe interrupted Cobie before she could speak and said, "Cobie, you do know that Cloe is almost an identical twin to you. She could be your younger sister. If she'd wash her face, she'd be almost as beautiful as you are."

"I've been told that she is my Mini Me more times than I can count. I thank God she looks like me instead of her long nosed father," a red faced Cobie replied.

"Mom, you changed the subject. I don't trust him. He says nice things and then uses a chainsaw on women and kids."

"Look, if you don't want to go just say so. I won't make you. Now finish eating and get your butt outside and bring some more limbs to the cabin to be sawed down to size," said Cobie in frustration with her strong-willed daughter.

"Cloe, I can carry most of the stuff by myself, so you can stay here and gather firewood all day," replied Joe, and then he added, "I'm not sure I trust you either. You could be one of those Islamic Terrorists in little girls disguise."

"Wait a darn minute. I'm not a little girl."

Joe sawed and stacked wood the rest of the day while Cloe packed the logs to the cabin and stacked it just outside the back door. He tried not to think about the raven-haired beauty in the cabin as he did his chores. He failed miserably.

"Joe. Joe. Hey, Joe, wake up! Mom said dinner would be ready in twenty minutes."

Joe was deep in thought about the woman in the cabin when Cloe hailed him, and he knew he had to get away from these two in the near future. They didn't need him when Cobie healed, and the Munchkin didn't want him around. He had learned the hard way not to cling to someone who didn't want you around.

"I'll finish this branch and then clean up for the day. Thanks for waking me up. I was daydreaming about before the bombs fell," Joe told the girl.

"Joe, you were awfully quiet this afternoon. Did I piss you off or sumptin?"

"No more than usual. You know your mom loves you and no one will ever come between you and her. One day a man will come into her life, and you don't want to make her choose between you and a man she loves. She will always choose you and will miss out on another part of her life," Joe said as they walked to the cabin.

Cobie handed them a bucket of water, washcloth, and soap as they walked up and said, "Today is the day you two start cleaning up outside. Start by sweeping the sawdust off each other and then wash up for supper. Hurry up the water is warm," Cobie said as she looked at the dirty pair.

"Be careful lifting," Joe said.

"I'm only using my good arm," Cobie said.

Cobie surprised them with rabbit roasted over the fire in addition to rabbit stew when they joined her at the table. They were all full to their eyes with rabbit stew and at least the roasted rabbit was a bit different.

"I wish we had some more vegetables to go in the stew," moaned Cloe as she played with her spoon in the stew.

"I might be able to rustle up a few cans of vegetables when I go to my cabin tomorrow. That does bring up the question of a trip into town to try to find more food. I'm not a dietitian but only eating meat every day and a few canned vegetables can't be good over the long haul. A little girl needs vegetables, vitamins, carbs, and other stuff that's good for them," Joe said.

"I'm not a little girl," Cloe protested.

"Then start acting like a young lady," her mom answered.

"Back to the topic at hand, I plan to go to my home tomorrow and bring some supplies back here. I will then go back to my cabin so I can get an early start to the city. I will sleep most of the afternoon and evening tomorrow so I can leave for the city before midnight. I want to be in and out of the city before daylight. I need a list of anything you really need before I get back here tomorrow morning," Joe told the girls.

"Joe is it worth risking your life over a can of green beans," Cobie asked with a frown on her face.

"No, but I need a few crucial items and might as well fetch some other things. I'm going to hit the hospital and doctor's offices to find some antibiotics and other medical supplies. I don't plan to risk my life. I won't confront anyone, and I don't plan on becoming a hero or a statistic in this disaster," Joe insisted.

The next morning, Joe had breakfast with the girls and then headed to his cabin. He took a southern route this time to avoid wearing a path. He stopped at the edge of the woods before walking across a small open area, looked around for danger, and didn't see any. Joe was halfway across the meadow when he saw a place where the grass was matted down. He looked around, saw something shiny, and picked it up. He was holding a folding knife in his hand that wasn't rusty because it had been lost only a short time ago. Joe now knew people were wondering across his property. He pushed on toward his cabin and stopped a short distance from it while still hidden by the woods.

He watched, listened, and then approached the cabin. He didn't see any signs of footprints in the sand around the cabin and felt much relieved. Joe gathered a bag full of canned vegetables, a few boxes of pasta, and the spices. He cut a generous portion of venison from the haunch and placed the food on the table.

Joe walked over to the kitchen table and read several of the group of letters that he was supposed to read every day and quickly read them. His Grandma had a quick wit but could also use sarcasm like a knife. He picked up another that read:

Dear Joe:

Have you thought much about prepping yet? The cabin is a nice one but has none of the modern conveniences. It was our Bugout place and was meant to give Grandpa and me a place where we could survive an apocalypse.

We were always worried about Russia or China attacking at first, and then the damn Iranians and North Koreans got the bomb thanks to our weak assed presidents. When the Bitcoin bubble burst ten years ago, the entire financial system almost failed. Thank God, the president back in 2019 made it illegal to use the fake money in the USA. The USA prospered as the rest of the world went into a depression. We dodged that apocalypse.

When Eastern Europe became part of the Caliphate in 2022, quick action by the US military kept Great Britain, France, and Italy from falling into the terrorist's hands. I know the wars in Europe will go on way past your lifetime but could eventually lead to an apocalypse.

You should get the picture that I'm painting is that the world is going to crap and half of our country is helping the bastards ruin it. Read the survival books in the basement and become a survivor.

Yep, that's tough talk, but I'm a tough old broad. Do what I said and you will live. Be prepared to do the hard stuff. It will soon be a kill or be killed world out there.

Love Grandma.

Joe didn't laugh as he read the letter this time and vowed to read all of the survival books. He took the next five letters and put them in his backpack. He then went down to the basement and brought up an arm full of the books. He sorted through the books and decided to take the books titled Army Survival Manual FM 21-76, Edible Wild Plants, The Ultimate Survival Medicine Guide, and Wilderness Survival Skills with him to read at Cobie's cabin.

Joe saw his compound bow setting in the corner and attached it to his backpack along with an assortment of arrows. He planned to practice using the bow at Cobie's cabin and thought he would look for a bow for women during one of his trips into town.

He locked the cabin and started his trek back to the other cabin deep in thought about what his Grandma had warned. He wondered how his grandparents had led such a happy life while being so paranoid. It dawned on him that by being prepared for whatever life threw at them made them happy. Knowing that you have food and weapons set aside along with the skills to survive had a very calming effect on people. He felt just the opposite and vowed to do what it took to obtain that calm feeling from being prepared.

He approached the cabin and Bennie greeted him even though the dog was tied to the side of the porch with his muzzle around his snout. He stopped long enough to rub Bennie's ears and noticed Bennie had several cuts on his head and side. The dog was okay, so he walked up on the porch, set his gear down, and knocked on the door.

"Hey, it's me, Joe. Can I come in?"

The door opened, and both Cobie and Cloe almost knocked him down trying to hug him. They were both scared and clung to him as he tried to set his bags down on the floor.

"Girls, what happened to scare you fearless women?"

"This morning Cloe went outside to see why Bennie was barking and walked into a group of hungry Coyotes. They were trying to eat Bennie, and Cloe scared them off with two shots from her pistol. Poor Bennie got some bites and scratches but will be okay," said Cobie.

"When I get back from town, I'll hunt them down and thin them out. Coyotes usually don't attack humans but will eat a dog or rabbits. They will raid our traps, and we'll never have game to eat," said Joe.

"Do you have to go to town? Those little monsters scared the crap out of Cloe and me. We were afraid that they would get in the cabin and eat us," replied Cobie.

"Hey, throw Cloe outside next time they show up. One bite off that sour girl will run the Coyotes over to Idaho," he laughed.

"Joe we are scared. Why aren't you taking this seriously," asked Cobie?

"Hey, I'm sorry, but it was weird to see the little girl who killed a terrorist and stuck a gun in my face afraid of a few wild dogs. I promise I'll get rid of them when I get back from town. I'm going to break out my bow and hunt them down silently," Joe said.

Cloe asked, "Do you have a bow and arrows?"

"Yes, they are on the porch. I've never used one much and want to learn how to hunt with one. Bows are silent and will never run out of ammunition," replied Joe.

"Could you teach me how to shoot one," the young girl asked?"

"I will, but you have to do something first," Joe said as he pulled a small book out of his backpack then said, "Read this book on how to bow hunt and be ready for lessons when I get back."

Cloe took the book and sat down by the fire to read the book. Joe and Cobie went into the kitchen with the bags and began to unload them so Cobie could put them away.

"Joe, I can't thank you enough for bringing the spices and food back to us. You were right about all of us needing the vegetables. Oh, look a bottle of vitamins," Cobie said as she placed the items in their proper place.

"I got them when I went into town. I kept a bottle at my place, so you and Cloe take them. I will get more tomorrow. I'm glad to help out and can't wait for more home cooking."

Cobie dug down in the last bag and was delighted to find women's makeup, more feminine hygiene products, and shampoo. She gave Joe a hug and said, "I guess you were tired of looking at us old hags with dirty faces and no makeup."

"Cobie, you are a beautiful woman and don't need makeup. I just got it because women like that sort of stuff," he replied.

Cobie brought him close and kissed him on the cheek then said, "Joe, you are a good man, and I thank God every day that he brought you into our lives."

This caught Joe off guard, and he quickly backed away and said, "Well, I have to go back to the cabin and get some rest before heading out to the city tonight. You and Cloe need to stay in the cabin if possible until I get back. Goodbye," he said as he headed out the door.

Cobie watched as he patted Cloe on the back and said goodbye to her as he walked away. She was sad until he turned to look back at her and he smiled before walking away. She didn't know what was going on in this man's mind but she knew someone had hurt him deeply and he was guarding himself against further pain by avoiding women as much as possible. The thought struck her that they were very much alike.

☆

Chapter 12

Joe slept all afternoon and didn't wake up until 6:00 pm when the old windup alarm clock rang out. It was dark outside, and by leaving early, he could scavenge for several more hours. He felt rested and ready to go as he slipped into his clothes and shouldered his gear. He would hike down to the quarry and drive the Jeep down the mountain to a hiding spot then hike into town. He would use the Jeep to store his loot until it was full, and then return to the cabin. He planned to hide the Jeep in a storage unit by the Airport and use it as his base of operation. Joe took the bulbs from the on the Jeep to make sure he didn't draw unwanted attention to his drive and checked the vehicle for anything that rattled.

Joe pulled away from the quarry with no headlights to decrease the chance of being seen. This time he took back roads and ATV paths down the hills to the town. He had a few scary moments when he struck a small tree stump and was stuck in a ravine for a few minutes but otherwise made it safely down the hill.

He stopped to look over the storage sheds and the area around it for movement and other dangers. He watched while he ate a small can of chicken and then drove into the storage complex. He found an empty shed on the end facing the street and backed the Jeep into the shed. Joe took his empty backpack and a duffel bag with him as he moved to an abandoned house across the street that had a good view of the unit he left the Jeep inside. He waited for half an hour waiting to see if anyone followed him before he felt safe enough to move on.

After making sure all of his equipment was well hidden, he moved out toward the houses. He cut through the subdivision to reach the Highway 5 overpass and noticed there were no lights on in any direction he looked. There was some sporadic gunfire off in the distance, which made him very nervous. Joe saw many signs of intense firefights with bullet holes in houses and shell casings everywhere. The second week after the lights went out saw neighbor killing neighbor to steal food. Then the gangs took over and killed anyone who wouldn't join them or just for grins and giggles. There was no law, but the gun in your hand and the guns were used liberally.

He walked under the Highway 5 overpass and saw several dead men and women. The women had their clothes torn off, and the men had been executed. Someone had spray painted the Star of David on their chests. These animals had also mutilated their bodies. The scene deeply angered Joe, and he vomited several times as he continued to move on into town. The depravity of mankind had been unchained by the EMP blasts, and it appeared that morality and law enforcement was a thing of the past.

Joe now knew that he was right about hiding in the woods and becoming self-sufficient to stay away from this mess in the cities. He wished he didn't have to make the runs into the town and vowed that once his crops came in, he would never go into the city again. He also knew that if he were discovered, he would probably have to kill or be killed.

Highway 66 was strewn with wrecked and burned cars, but he saw no signs of life as he walked along in the shadows heading west. Joe saw a small sporting goods store on the left side in a strip mall. He cautiously entered the store and saw it had been looted. Every gun and knife had been taken, but he noticed a small display of bows in the back. He found a lighter pull bow for Cloe and attached it to his backpack. He added a quiver and filled it with arrows, and then moved on up the street staying close to the buildings.

There was an animal clinic on the right up ahead, and Joe remembered that many animal drugs were the same as human medicines. He slid in behind the building and saw the door had been broken off the hinges. That wasn't a good sign, but he hoped the looters were looking for prescription painkillers and not medicine.

The office was a wreck and had been looted several times. The locked cage where the Veterinarian stored the prescription drugs had the door smashed, and bottles of pills and loose pills were scattered all over the floor. Joe took a broom and dustpan, swept the pills together, and placed them in a bag. He then searched through the bottles and found several with drug names that sounded familiar. He filled his backpack and duffel bag with all the drugs he thought were worth taking. He added several bottles of rubbing alcohol, bandages, and other assorted medical items to his bags.

Joe was thankful all of the animal cages were empty because he had dreaded the thought of animals starving to death. He walked toward the front office when he spied a door on his right. He opened the door to see a huge mess of office and janitorial supplies. He sorted through them and selected a bundle of copy paper and a package of various colored marking pens for Cloe and a six-pack of toilet paper.

He then searched the desks in the front office and found nothing of value. Joe then moved to the Vet's office and found several books on animal medicine and a copy of The Pill Book, which appeared to explain about many medications and what they do. He thought that perhaps Cobie would know something about the animal drugs and hoped most could be used for humans. As he was about to leave he saw a metal First Aid cabinet on the wall and emptied the contents into his backpack along with a First Aid book that was in a rack below the enclosure. Joe didn't see anything else worth taking and headed back to the Jeep to unload his bags and start scavenging again.

He went back through a different part of the subdivision and noticed the gunfire sounded much closer to his position. He saw several dead bodies that were outside of a house. The windows were smashed in and bullet holes riddled the area around the front door. Joe heard something across the street and dove into the bushes beside the front porch. It was very dark under the canopy of shrubs as Joe crawled toward an opening to see what had made the noise.

Joe saw two young men with AR-15s in their hands and sawed-off shotguns hanging from slings over their shoulders. They were talking as they scanned the houses along their walk.

"I know those Muslims are back in town tonight. Big John wants them dead, and he will reward us if we bring a dead one to him," the short one said.

"I don't know. Let's find a hiding spot and then go back to the crib in the morning. We ain't heroes. You saw what those camel jockeys did to that carload of Jews. I don't want no part of them. John needs to get off the drugs and help us get the fuck away from those animals," said the tall one.

They kept talking as they walked on up the street, but Joe couldn't make out what they were saying. Joe knew all Muslims weren't bad but then on the other hand he knew most terrorists these days were Islamic and that meant Muslim to Joe. Joe wasn't into politics and just wanted people to stop killing other people.

The men were out of sight, and Joe sat still for a few minutes more to make sure they were gone. He sat under the bush with a strange feeling that something was wrong around him. It was pitch dark under the bush, and he didn't hear anything. Then it dawned on him that the smell of a scented soap had caught his senses. He stayed very still for a minute and didn't take a breath. He was right. He heard someone or something breathing close to him.

Joe said, "I'm not going to hurt you, but if you don't show yourself I'm going to let loose with this shotgun."

"Don't move or I'll pull this trigger," a voice in the dark said.

"Look, I'm just hiding from those men and don't want to hurt anyone. Just take your finger off the trigger, and I'll leave," said Joe with fear in his voice as he slowly pointed his pistol at where the voice came from.

"I followed you from the Vet's office, and I need some of those drugs for my husband. Give me that bag, and I'll let you go."

"No, I won't do that, but I will share them with you. I have a sick daughter who needs antibiotics. Do you know what your husband needs? What happened to him," Joe asked.

"That gang chased a man close to where we were hiding, and a stray bullet hit him in the thigh. Do you know any first aid? I did the best I could, but I can't stand the sight of blood," the lady said.

"How far away is he," Joe asked the lady.

"Maybe a quarter mile west. We have a hideout in a building north of that self-storage lot on Highway 66."

She pointed southwest and said, "It's that way a couple of blocks."

"Okay, I'll share my meds with you and take a look at your husband. Do you have anything to trade? I need some vitamins, soap, and women's stuff," Joe said as he struggled to remember Cobie's list.

"We have some extras of those. Follow me," the woman said as she stood up behind the bushes, and then added, "The gangs patrol on foot, but the Arabs drive military vehicles.

170

They like to fool people into thinking they are the US Army and kill or capture anyone who approach them."

The woman stuck to the shadows close to buildings as much as possible as she worked her way to their hideout. She led him to a building north of the self-storage units. She walked up to a building that had been half burned down and slipped around to the backside where she moved a couple of charred boards and went into the blackness below. Joe followed her when a light illuminated the floor ahead. There were burned chairs, boards, and ashes piled along their path until they turned a corner. She knocked three times on the door and then opened it to reveal a room lit by a kerosene lantern. There were several adults and children in the room. One of the women raised a knife when she saw Joe enter the room.

"Jane put the knife down. He is here to help us."

Joe stared at the lady who had convinced him to help her husband. He turned to the lady with the knife and said, "You had better get something besides a knife if you want to stay alive out there. Now let's take a look at your husband's leg."

The man was asleep on top of a stack of boxes with his leg propped up. Joe pulled the blanket back and saw the wound appeared to be recent.

"Can you boil some water to help sterilize my knife and whatever else I'm going to use to get the bullet out? The bullet must have hit something else, or it would have gone clean through the fleshy part of his leg. Give him these Ibuprofen pills. Thank God, it's on the outside just above the knee. I'll dig it out and give you some of my antibiotics to keep the infection down. Jane, take this book and find the section on puncture or gunshot wounds and read it aloud," Joe said.

"Hey, what are your names?"

"I'm Ginny West, and Dan is my husband. We're from California and were up here on vacation with Jane and her family. Her boyfriend Bill left to find help yesterday and hasn't come back yet," the lady responded.

"I'm Joe, and I … err live a ways from here and scavenge in town every now and then."

Joe turned to look at Jane and saw tears flowing as she tried to keep her children calm. Jane began reading from the First Aid book while Joe examined a pile of their tools to find something to pull the bullet from Dan's leg. He saw a pair of needle nose pliers and gave his knife and the pliers to Ginny to sterilize in the pan full of water heating on a camp stove.

He looked around the room and saw Jane, her two teenaged boys, and Ginny and her teenaged girl and boy. All were dirty and malnourished. He now had an inner battle going on in his mind with an angel fighting a little red devil over if he should help them. He knew he could provide for himself and maybe the girls back at the cabin but seven more people could cause them all to starve or worse. They could cause him to be discovered. He felt like crap thinking about abandoning them when they had so much need. There had to be a solution he could live with. Then he asked himself what would Grandma do?

Joe listened to what Jane repeated from the book as he thought about a solution to helping these people when a noise pulled him from his thoughts.

"Joe. Hey Joe," Jane said twice before Joe turned then added, "The water has been boiling for twenty minutes. The instruments should be clean."

Joe took them from the boiling water, rinsed them in alcohol before he turned to Dan's leg, and said, "I need all of you to hold him down. Those pain pills will dull the pain, but this is going to hurt."

They held him down, and Joe used the needle nose pliers to probe the wound to see how deep the bullet was and was pleasantly surprised that it was only an inch below the surface. He slowly opened the pliers to grab the bullet when Dan woke up and screamed. His wife quickly placed her hand over his mouth, and they all kept him from moving. Joe felt the ends of the pliers around the bullet and pulled it out. Dan shook violently as the pain shot through his leg.

"Hold him still while I put pressure on the wound to stop the bleeding. I think Jane said to leave it open and apply the antibiotic salve. Your husband will be fine in a couple of weeks. Now I'm tired and need to crash. Wake me up if anyone approaches," Joe said.

Before Joe went to sleep, he pulled the day's letter from his Grandma out to read.

Dear Joe:

Joe, I'm very sick today, and my doctor is a pain in my butt. I talked to you earlier today, and your voice made my day. I hope my letters bring some good to your day and perhaps a smile every now and then. Have you started the treasure hunt yet? You are a bright boy and can figure it out.

I'm tired. I think I'll take a nap after Alfred reads to me. I don't want to shock you but a couple of years after your Grampa died Alfred and I got close. Real close. Were both too old to do much in bed now but he was the second love of my life.

As the youngsters say these days – make that picture go away.

Bet you're laughing now!

Love Grandma.

Joe thought what treasure hunt then remembered their walks and burying small boxes.

Joe slept until just after dark that evening until they heard glass breaking from outside the door. Jane said, "Someone just entered the hallway. Grab your knives. Joe, wake up!"

Joe put his boots on and handed Ginny his .22 pistol then said, "You have ten shots. Use them wisely."

He took his hunting knife from its sheath, drew his 9mm pistol with his right hand, and walked out the door to confront the invader. He walked out into the hallway and hid in a room waiting inside to see who was intruding on the hideout. He saw a light dash across the wall opposite the room he was in and heard two people whispering.

"I know I hear someone yelling from dis building."

"You hearing shit."

"Fuck you. Follow me, and we'll take hostages back to da boss."

"Screw dat. We'll kill them and take their stuff unless it's some young sweet thing."

Joe waited behind the door until the two shined their light into the room he was hidden in and moved on. He cautiously walked up behind the trailing man and froze in place when the two stopped. His sense of smell had sharpened since living in the woods. He could smell the stench of perspiration and urine coming off the two gangbangers. He wondered if this was normal for the two or if they had lost their desire to stay clean after the missiles fell.

"There, I done told you I hear something. There's a woman's voice in the room up ahead. We gonna get some tail tonight."

The men moved toward Joe's new friends with guns in hand. Joe ripped his knife across the trailing man's throat dropping him to the ground. The other man turned around shooting at Joe as Joe slashed his blade into the man's side. The man tried to kill Joe with his rifle but was too close, and the blade was working deeper into the man's gut. Joe ripped the blade deep across the man's stomach and felt the man's bowels slide across his hand on the way to the floor. The smell of the feces struck Joe hard, as he knew the shit was on his gloves.

As the man died and fell to the floor, the thug squeezed the trigger, fired one shot, which grazed Joe on the side of his hip. Joe took off his gloves and pushed his free hand down hard on his wound to stop the bleeding. The pressure made the wound sting like hell.

Joe searched the men and found two cheap Hi-point 9mm pistols, a Ruger Mini 14, and a Mossberg pump shotgun. He found several extra magazines for the guns and a pocket full of 00-Buck shotgun shells. He took the weapons with him and went back to the room where his new friends were hidden.

Joe's hands shook as he knocked on the door and said, "It's me, Joe. The danger is over, but we need to get out of here quickly."

"You smell like shit," the dark-haired woman said.

"One of the men had an accident. I need to clean up and change clothes," Joe responded.

He handed a pistol to Ginny, gave the shotgun to Jane, and said, "Do you know how to use these?

They all said yes, and then Ginny said, "We can't leave now Dan can't walk. Besides, where would we go? What happened to the people trying to get in? Did they go away?"

Joe looked at the kids and said, "Something like that. Those two won't bother anyone anymore. Trust me that gunshot will bring the gang over here in a few minutes. I'll take you somewhere safe. Ginny, help me support Dan as we walk to my Jeep. I'll take you to a cabin up in the hills where you will be safe."

Jane saw Joe holding his hip and pushed his hand away.

"Joe, you got shot," Jane said as she tended to his wound.

Jane made him drop his pants to the floor, and she flushed the wound with hydrogen peroxide. She then dabbed antibiotic cream on the wound and bandaged it.

"Ginny, Joe is right. We've almost been discovered twice before. We need to get out of this horrible town. Bill is dead, and he won't be coming back. We've waited too long for him," Jane said as she finished tending to Joe.

"Okay let's do it. Kids grab our bags. Butch, you get the stove, and Dot, grab one of the lanterns," Ginny said.

Joe washed off the best he could and put on some of Dan's clothes. He was now ready to travel. They snuck out of their home for the past several weeks and left. Ginny and Joe helped Dan walk using only his good leg. It was just 150 yards to the storage unit where the Jeep was hidden. Joe opened the roll up door and ushered everyone inside. He watched for the gang while he instructed the others to tie their possessions and his bags to the roof and back of the Jeep.

"Look it's going to be tight, and you will have to sit on each other's laps for about an hour, but we will get the hell out of here and to a safe place," Joe told the group.

They quickly finished squeezing everyone into the Jeep and Ginny opened the overhead door. Joe drove away from the storage lot with his lights off and headed across several open fields to Emigrant Creek Road where he took a right turn. He drove a short distance and then drove cross-country up into the hills for a mile before he stopped to look at one of his maps.

Joe had mixed feelings about what to do with the people because he couldn't leave them behind but didn't want them in one of his cabins. He looked at one of the maps his

Grandma left for him and saw his cabins circled and several others a few miles away. He decided he would take them to one of the other cabins and hope it was unoccupied. He drove through woods and clearings until he found a forest service road and took it for a mile in the direction he needed to travel. He went off the road again for half a mile and arrived at a spot close to the first cabin, which was half a mile southeast of the southwest corner of his property.

He parked the Jeep several hundred feet from where the cabin was located on the map. He told the others to stay in the Jeep and keep quiet while he checked things out. He had missed the cabin in the dark, and he was forced to backtrack to find it. He was surprised to see an older cabin behind a modern looking cabin. There was no one around, and he searched until he found a key hidden under a fake rock by the porch. Joe let himself into the cabin. The cabin was beautiful on the inside and was much more attractive than his home. Joe took a quick tour of the place and was surprised to see the cabinets held several days' worth of food.

Joe walked back to the Jeep and drove to the new cabin. Everyone piled out of the Jeep and headed inside. Joe sat Dan on the couch and started a fire in the fireplace.

"This is your new home, and I need to leave you with some rules for staying alive. Don't have a fire in the daytime. There are bad people north of here, and they might see the smoke. Don't make any loud noises. Saw the firewood. Never chop it with an ax, because that would make too much noise. You have enough food to last until I return in a day or two. Please stay close to the cabin until I return. Oh, I'm leaving the shotgun and two pistols with you. I need the Mini 14."

"Joe, please stay with us," Jane pleaded.

"I have to get back to my family. I was supposed to return yesterday, so I know they are worried. If you do what I just said, you will be okay. I'm leaving the Jeep behind the old cabin. Do not use it unless it is to escape an attack. I plan to leave it here and use it for scavenging trips into town. I need to go now," Joe said as he shouldered his backpack and lifted his carry bag.

"Where is your home," Ginny asked.

"It's about five miles away," Joe answered as he walked in the opposite direction of the cabin. He liked these people but trusted no one.

Joe walked the mile and a quarter to his cabin and unloaded half of the medical supplies and his rifle, choosing to carry the Mini 14 since it was a semiautomatic and had three 20 round magazines. He selected several cans of vegetables, a bottle of vitamins, and then hiked to Cobie's cabin.

☆

Chapter 13

It was after midnight when Joe arrived at Cobie's cabin. He dropped his bags and gear on the porch, and then rested his back against the cabin wall. He didn't want to wake the girls up or scare them, so he planned to sleep on the porch until dawn. He had barely fallen asleep when he opened his eyes and saw that beautiful face a few feet from his.

"Joe, why are you on the porch? Come on in the house. Cloe, grab his gear. Joe when you didn't get home we were scared to death something had happened to you. Are you okay?"

"A lot happened in the past two days, but I'm okay. I met a family and helped them. I also met two gangbangers and ruined their day. I'm sorry, but I only made one run to the Vet's office before my day went to crap," Joe said as he stumbled getting up.

Cobie placed her arm around him to help steady him when she felt the cold sticky blood seep through her t-shirt. She helped him to a kitchen chair and told Cloe to light the lantern. She saw that the wet spots on Joe's hip and her side was his blood.

"Joe you've been wounded. Were you shot," Cobie fearfully asked?

"Yep, one of the punks got off a lucky shot and got me in the hip. One of the ladies doctored it for me," Joe answered.

"What ladies?" Cobie asked.

"Oh, there was a man, his wife, and two kids plus another woman and her two boys. I took them to a cabin about a mile away to help them get out of town. It's real bad in town," he said.

"Take your pants off and drop your shorts enough so I can get to your wound," Cobie ordered.

"I'm okay."

"You heard what I said. Do it now," Cobie said with resolve then added, "or I'll kick your ass."

Joe needed help standing, and Cobie took his pants off and laid him on the couch. She pulled his shorts down on the wounded side, cleaned the wound, and applied more of the antibiotic salve. She then placed a wad of gauze on top of the three-inch-long gash. She kept the pressure on it for fifteen minutes until it stopped bleeding. Joe fell asleep, and Cobie gently lowered him until his head was on a pillow. She covered him with his sleeping bag and sat up with him the rest of the night while Cloe went back to bed.

Cloe woke up an hour before daybreak and saw her mom placing a log on the fire. She looked over at Joe and for the first time wanted him to stay in their lives. He had taught her a lot about trapping, hunting, and survival and she wanted to continue the lessons. Cloe knew she had to be kinder to Joe or he would eventually get mad and leave them alone. She noticed that Joe wasn't asleep and that he watched her mom through squinted eyes.

"Good morning mom, how is your patient doing?"

"I think he's okay. He'll need some pain pills when he wakes up, but the bullet just made a gash in his hip," her mom replied.

"Mom, can you teach me how to care for people? Mr. Harp has been good to us, and I'd hate to think something bad could happen to anyone of us, and I couldn't help them," Cloe asked.

"I'd be glad to. We'll start with you reading the first chapter in the First Aid manual, and I'll answer questions."

Joe's hip was throbbing with pain, and he said, "You can start by teaching her to give her patient some pain meds before his hip falls off."

Cloe fetched a bottle of Ibuprofen and handed Joe the pills while her mom poured a glass of water for him. Joe swung his feet around and sat up as he winced in pain so he could swallow the pills. He downed the pills with a swig of water and grinned to hide his pain.

"Joe, I'll fix some breakfast while you give us the details about your trip," Cobie said as she put coffee in the old coffee pot and started a fire in the cook stove.

Joe told them every detail except how he killed the punks who were going to attack him and those families; the girls didn't ask. They were happy that Joe had added to the medicine cabinet but were very happy to see more toilet paper, soap, and a bottle of dishwashing liquid.

"Joe it's amazing how most women wanted a diamond ring or fancy car before the lights went out and now I'm dancing for joy over toilet paper. I was never a high maintenance woman, and God knows we never had much, but we always had toilet paper and soap," Cobie said.

Cobie went outside to bring in a load of wood when Cloe walked over and sat on the couch by him.

"Joe, I'm sorry for being a brat at times. I was raised better than that," Cloe apologized.

"Cloe, you never hurt my feelings. I knew your world had been turned upside down and you were only adjusting to the new normal," Joe said.

"Joe, my mom worked her ass off to make sure I never knew we were poor. She sacrificed everything a woman would want, so I had decent clothes and a good school to attend. I'll never be able to pay her back. My mom is the best woman in the world," Cloe said with tears in her eyes.

Joe pulled the young teen close and said, "You are a good person, and that means more than anything else to your mom. She loves you more than her own life, and all you have to do to repay her is to keep being the good person you are. If you grow up to be half the person your mom is then you will be one hell of a good woman. You already are almost as beautiful as she is now."

Cobie had heard them talking and listened from the other side of the door. Tears came to her eyes. She was so proud of her daughter and liked the way Joe had made Cloe feel good about herself. She thought that maybe it was about time for Cloe to have a father figure in her life.

"Joe, when do we meet these people and why didn't you bring them here," Cobie asked as she entered the cabin.

"Cobie, your number one job is to protect your daughter. We don't know these people. Even good people are killing for food these days, and they were starving when I found them. I think they are the kind of people we want to have around us, but I still don't want them to know where our homes are until I can get to know them better," Joe replied.

"Is the lady single?"

"Yes and no. Jane's boyfriend left to find medical supplies and never returned. That is why they stayed so long in the city hoping he would return," he explained.

"How old are their kids? Are any my age? Can we go see them today?" Cloe asked in a barrage of questions.

"Oh, I'd guess they run from sixteen down to about your age. The kids were all scared and very timid when I saw them. Ginny's husband had been shot in the leg, and that forced them to scavenge for food. They weren't very good at it either.

184

I want to observe them for a day or so before I take you two over there. Safety first has to be our motto these days. I'm starving let's eat," Joe said.

They ate breakfast and then Joe took Cloe outside and showed her the new bow. He took the time to teach her the basics of shooting a bow and let her pull the bowstring back and shoot several arrows before telling her they had to run the traps.

He followed Cloe while she checked the rabbit traps. His leg was in pain, which caused him to limp. The limping as he walked caused other muscles to get sore, but he sucked it up and finished the route without complaining. The improved techniques he had taught Cloe had doubled their harvest. They found six rabbits in the traps and Cloe was happy until they got to the last trap and found a half-eaten carcass.

"Couldn't we raise rabbits in a caged in area and save a bunch of time walking around the forest?" she asked.

"That's a darn good idea once we can grow some rabbit food in our garden," Joe answered.

"I'll bet no one has stolen rabbit food from the Co-op store. We need to find books on raising rabbits and other animals. We probably could raise goats, they'll eat anything," the girl proudly said.

Cloe was right, and Joe needed to unleash their brainpower. He knew he had to either bring a hundred books to them or take them to his real home. He thought they were living together now and he knew he could trust them. He decided to ask them to move in with him, and they could start becoming a family if Cobie agreed.

"Cloe, I'll make a run to the Co-op to bring some rabbit fencing, lumber, and rabbit food back, so you can start rabbit ranching. I'll teach you how to make a trap to catch the little varmints alive and make you responsible for the entire process," he said.

"That would be totally awesome," I'll become the Bill Gates or Steve Jobs of rabbit ranching. I'll call my company "The Bunny Ranch.""

"You might want to check with your mom on the name. She might want some input. Let's head back to the cabin and make a couple of the box traps if I can find some flat boards.

Cloe started to complain about having to skin the rabbits when Joe reminded her that half of the bunny ranching was harvesting and skinning the varmints. She cleaned the rabbits while Joe went about finding nails, wood, and something to cut or drill a hole in the top of the box.

Joe went to Cobie and said, "Cloe wants to start raising rabbits for food. I hope you don't mind, but I told her it would be okay and I would get what she needs to get started."

"That's great. I'm sick and tired of rabbit stew, fried rabbit, and roasted rabbit but it sure beats starving. Why the concerned look on your face?" Cobie asked.

"She wants to name her new company "The Bunny Ranch."

"Oh, after the Playboy Bunnies?"

"No, she is too innocent to know about the Bunny Ranch outside of Las Vegas that sells female companionship to men," he laughed as he replied.

"Oh crap, that is too funny. I like the name and the double meaning. No one will tell her, and she will get lots of strange looks," she laughed.

"So, we will start the Bunny Ranch Empire as soon as I can go to the Co-Op and get the supplies we need. Cloe let me know that we should be raising goats and other animals. I have hundreds of books back at my cabin, and we'll make a trip there to see what we can learn about raising animals. We'll visit my place after we visit the new folks. I would like you to think about moving in with me. It is better insulated and has solar powered lights and running water from a well," Joe said.

"How is your hip? I'll bet it still hurts a lot," Cobie said.

"The pain meds take the edge off. I'm okay," Joe answered.

"Honestly, I was beginning to think that you didn't have a cabin and had just moved in with us," Cloe laughed as she replied then added, "Joe I like you, but I have to think about that for a bit before making that decision."

This struck Joe the wrong way, and he felt she didn't get it that he owned the cabins, and she was the one being allowed to stay in his other cabin. He felt she should have jumped at the chance of moving to a nicer cabin. He didn't respond and went to see how Cloe was progressing on the rabbits. He walked up and saw Cloe feeding rabbit guts to her dog. He also saw the pile of rabbit fur that would be tossed.

"Cloe, add tanning rabbit fur to your new company's portfolio. I'm sure I have some books that cover tanning hides. Now take the meat to your mom, and we will get on with building our first trap to catch live rabbits," Joe told the girl.

The traps were merely wooden boxes about a foot square by three feet long. He installed a door that dropped down from above with the other end closed. He had cut a hole in the top of the box about four inched from the closed end to allow the trigger stick to poke down into the box. He then nailed an upright board on the top of the box for the swing arm. The trigger was a stick with a notch about four inches from the bottom with a sharp end to hold the bait. The trigger and door were held by a string at opposite ends of the box. When the rabbit nudged the food on the end of the trigger it moved and allowed the door on the other end of the swing arm to fall trapping the rabbit in the box.

Joe made the first box while Cloe and Cobie watched, and then watched while the girls made the second box. It was now close to suppertime, so Cobie went to prepare supper while the other two cleaned up and put away their tools and the rabbit traps.

Joe checked his backpack and oiled his new Mini 14 while he waited on supper to be ready. He showed Cloe how to field strip her pistol, clean, and oil it when he was through with his. Cobie saw him preparing his gear and asked, "Are you getting ready for tomorrow?"

"I thought I'd hike over to the new group and see what they are doing. I want to observe them when they think no one is around,"

Cobie thought for a minute and asked, "Don't you think spying on them is an intrusion of their privacy?"

"Yes it is, but if they want to live near us, we need to feel comfortable that they aren't going to harm us or become a problem," he replied.

Cobie asked, "Are you this paranoid about everyone who enters Mr. Harp's world?"

"I think of it as being cautious and performing due diligence. Cobie, many people who were nice before, will do anything to feed their families. I gave them enough food for three days, and now I want to make sure they are friendly," Joe said.

"So you would do that with anyone entering your world? I guess you checked us out as well," Cobie asked as her anger rose.

"Cobie don't get your panties in a wad. Yes, I checked you out to make sure there were no others with you and that I could trust you. It would be insane not to," Joe replied as he noticed the topic had angered her.

"So did you get an eye full? Were we naked like your tramp when you watched us," Cobie asked as she slammed the door and walked out of the cabin?

Cloe looked at Joe then ran to her mother's side. Cobie wouldn't speak to Joe as he tried to calm her down, so he left to check out the other group. He couldn't understand why she was mad or why she couldn't understand his extreme caution. He thought about how to apologize but didn't know he'd done anything that needed an apology.

Joe staked out the cabin for a few hours as his new friends settled down for the night and only heard regular chit chat. He felt terrific when he listened to the adults telling the kids to thank the kind man for helping them. He gave up when the lantern went out and headed back to the cabin.

Joe knocked on the cabin door before entering and saw Cloe standing in the shadows with her pistol aimed at him.

"Oh, Joe, I'm so glad you are back. Mom's asleep. Why is she so mad at you for being cautious?

"Baby girl, I don't know, but I would do anything to make her stop being mad at me. I'll wait and see if she thinks it over and understands why we must be extremely cautious," he replied as he sent her to bed.

Joe slept fitfully that night and had terrible dreams about Cobie and Cloe disappearing from his life. He woke up before dawn, as usual, to see Cobie heading to the bathroom while Cloe started a fire in the cook stove. Joe threw a couple of logs on the fireplace to warm the room up and then dressed.

"Good morning Cloe. How are you today?"

"I'm good. Did you sleep well last night?"

"Not too good. I had a lot on my mind," he replied.

Cobie walked out of the restroom, and Joe said, "Good morning Cobie. I think this is going to be a great day."

"What's so good about it," Cobie tersely replied.

"Well, for starters I think we should go over this morning to visit with our new neighbors and take some supplies with us," he said in a gentle voice.

"So your peeping Tom trip last night was successful. I guess they met your approval so now they can be around us defenseless women," Cobie replied sarcastically.

"Cobie that was uncalled for. I don't know what is bothering you, but I've been nothing but helpful to you and

190

Cloe. I'm sorry that your world fell apart, but you'd better get over whatever the hell is stuck in your craw," Joe said with a red face.

"Or what. Are you going to throw us out of the cabin because it belongs to you? Well you're not my lord and master, and you can go screw yourself," Cobie said as tears ran down her face.

"Cobie, I'm not sorry for being cautious, and you can stay here as long as you want to stay. I'll move back to my cabin today after I visit the neighbors. You can come along or stay here. I'm leaving in two hours," he replied.

Joe spent the next two hours packing and gathering the items needed to make rabbit snares and some fishing gear for their new friends. Cloe came to him several times begging him to stay with them, but Joe politely said no each time. The girl went from hating Joe to loving him in a few days and was devastated that her mother made him leave their home.

Cloe went to her mom who was in their bedroom and said, "Mom, let's go with Joe to meet these people. You and Joe should be able to get along well enough for that. Please."

"Cloe don't get involved in my discussion with Joe. He appears to be a nice man but has a dark side, and I don't know if I can trust him. We were doing very well alone for the last ten years and can live alone a while longer without Mr. Harp telling us what to do or spying on us. We will go meet these people, and I hope they are nice folks," Cobie whispered to her daughter.

Joe led the way to the cabin, and as usual, stopped a hundred yards from the cabin, and went ahead alone to make sure it was safe for them. He saw Ginny and the kids gathering firewood from the woods and waved to catch their attention. He then looked back only to see Cobie right behind him waving at the people up ahead.

"So, you don't have time to look for danger before barging in do you?" Joe asked.

"I don't need your permission to do anything, Mr. Harp. Now let's meet these people."

Cloe walked by Joe, shrugged her shoulders, and shook her head before she said, "I think she went crazy, but she's my mom."

They walked up to the front of the cabin where Dan sat in a chair, and the others gathered around. Joe began to introduce everyone, but Ginny said, "My goodness Joe what a great looking family you have."

Cobie interrupted her and said, "We're not his family, and just met him a couple of weeks ago. He has been very helpful to us."

"Oh, my mistake. I thought Joe had a wife and kids," Ginny replied.

Joe avoided the issue and said, "We dropped by to leave you some food and other supplies and to show you how to snare rabbits. I wanted to bring Cobie and Cloe Simms to meet you since we are all neighbors. They live about a mile and a half northeast of here," Joe said and then introduced everyone.

Cloe went off to the side with the other kids, and Cobie talked with Ginny on the porch. Jane asked Joe, "Didn't you say you had a daughter?"

"I told you that so you wouldn't want all of the drugs. I did take all of them to the girls, so I'm sorry if I deceived you," he said.

"I would have done the same. Hey, what is that chic pissed off about? Cobie was staring holes in you when Ginny thought she was your wife," Jane said.

"I think I pissed her off because I'm a bit paranoid and overprotective. I check out anyone around me to make sure they are friendly before I trust them. She was mad because I snuck down here to check on your group last night. I'm sorry if that pisses you off, but I want to make sure no one is going to harm me or anyone I care about," Joe said.

"Joe it's horrible that you have to feel you have to do that, but we should all be more like you and not worry so much about feelings. I will kill to protect my kids, and I for one, want to learn anything I can from you. Thanks for helping us," Jane said and gave Joe a hug.

Cobie saw Jane hug Joe and it upset her. Then she got mad at herself for being upset about a man she thought she didn't care for.

Later, everyone moved to the cabin and sat on the front porch sharing stories about their lives before the lights went dark and were ready to move on to another topic when Jane said, "Joe you haven't told us about your background. Tell us please?"

"It's pretty boring, and I'm a private person."

Jane took his arm and acted as if she was twisting it when he said, "Ouch if you're going to torture me I'll tell you my name, rank, and serial number. I'm from Murfreesboro, Tennessee and was an auto mechanic. My fiancee and best friend died in the same accident, and a few days later my Grandma died leaving me most of the land north of here. I moved here to start a new life, and here I am?"

Everyone was speechless after hearing his horrible story, but Jane probed by asking, "Joe you are smiling, so there must be more to the story because you have us in tears."

"I'm smiling because my Grandma died at 97 and was one of my best friends. She has done many things that will help all of us survive. My girlfriend and best friend were ... let's say enjoying themselves in the back seat of my Explorer in a thunderstorm when lightning hit a tree, and it fell on them. The car was crushed, and they died in each other's arms. Let's just be nice and say they were much more suited to each other than she and I were. We would have had a miserable life. I was glad she was out of my life but feel guilty about laughing about how they died. That's why I'm smiling. Now please don't ask anymore because I've said all I'm going to say about that," Joe said very solemnly.

Cloe moved closer and hugged Joe then said, "Joe, I'm so sorry you had to go through that alone. Is there anything we can do to make your life a bit brighter?"

Joe stood up and said, "Yes there is. Cloe, you need to just be yourself. The rest of you can all learn what it takes to survive and lead a long and healthy life. That would make me happy. Cobie you know the way back to your cabin. Cloe, please teach them how to catch rabbits. I'm heading home to rest up a bit. Cloe, I'll fetch the supplies for The Bunny Ranch and help you get started. I'll check on you from time to time. Goodbye," Joe said as he hugged Cloe and picked up his backpack and carry bag.

Jane said, "But Joe you just got here, and we want to get to know you better."

The new people all asked Joe to stay longer, but he replied, "I'll be back, but I don't want to wear out my welcome."

Cloe went to her mother and said, "I guess that's what you wanted."

Ginny overheard the comment and just shook her head as she went to join Jane and the kids where Cloe was to teach the rabbit snaring class.

Cobie sat on the porch with Dan and watched Cloe deftly teach the other how to provide food for their families. Dan said, "I'll bet you are very proud of your daughter. Did she learn how to trap in the Girl Scouts?"

"No, Joe taught her how to hunt, fish, and trap. She even cleans the animals and cuts them up to be cooked or smoked. She is becoming quite the outdoorswoman."

"Too bad Joe is withdrawing back into his own world. We could learn a lot from him. We owe our lives to him. He single-handedly killed two armed men who were trying to break into our hideout," Dan said as he watched her face.

"He told me he ran off two men. I'll bet he didn't kill them."

"Lady, we had to walk through the blood and guts to escape from our hideout. Joe took both armed men on with a knife because he didn't want gunshots to draw attention to our hideout. The man is a hero to us. I'm sorry that you two have had a spat, but I'd recommend you get over it and play nice," Dan said in a very calming voice.

☆

Chapter 14

Several days passed before Joe poked his head out of his cabin. He was in a crappy mood and went from sulking to being pissed at the world and didn't know why. He convinced himself it had nothing to do with that arrogant black haired bitch in the old cabin. He did know that he missed Cloe and Bennie a lot and wanted to go see them but first, he had to make another run down to Ashland for the stuff to make the rabbit cages. Cloe had become very special to him, and he wanted her to succeed with her Bunny Ranch.

He checked his backpack, cleaned all three guns, and strapped on his pistol belt before hiking south to get the Jeep parked at the new neighbors. The days were all above freezing now, and the weather was very dry for this time of the year. He knew there would be some grass bent but didn't want to leave muddy tracks for people to follow.

Before he left the cabin, he placed two of his Grandma's letters in his backpack and read the one for that day.

Dear Joe:

I'll bet you're still trying to get that last picture out of your head. Now, on to more important things, I'll bet your aunts and cousins are really pissed at me for leaving all the land to you. By now, they have figured out that I gave Alfred a lovely home in Oregon and a beach house in Florida. You know Alfred was 30 years younger than I was and earned every dime of what I left him.

I hope Alfred is lying on a beach with a hot chick that's thirty years younger than he is. He deserves a great life.

Well, the medicine fogs my mind, and I may not make much sense at times but never forget that you are very special to me.

Love Grandma.

Joe laughed and wondered how his Grandma kept the affair a secret so long. He wished his dad were there to fill him in on some of the new tidbits he had learned.

Joe covered the mile and a half to the neighbor's cabin and was surprised to see Cloe outside cutting firewood with their saw. He saw one of the boys skinning a rabbit and the others fetching wood from farther out in the woods.

"Hey Cloe," Joe hailed.

"Joe, I miss you," Cloe yelled as she ran up and hugged him.

"Is this the smart assed young lady that gave me hell for a week?" Joe teased.

"Yes, but I learned quickly that you were just trying to help me and not harm us," she said as she glared at her mom as she approached.

"You are a good person and Cloe I'll always be there for you," Joe hugged her as he replied.

"Joe, you can have your cabin back. We moved into the old cabin here so we won't inconvenience you any longer," Cobie said with a touch of arrogance.

"You didn't have to leave. It wasn't bothering me. What if the owner of these cabins shows up one day? Will you pack up and live in the forest? Oh, suit yourself miss independent. I didn't come here to see you anyway. Hey Dan," Joe said as he left Cobie and walked over to Dan.

"Good to see you, Joe. Can you sit a spell and tell me a bit, about what you plan to do about gardening and raising animals. Cloe told me you two had some good plans before her mom got the burr up her ass," Dan said.

"Dan, I have more than enough seeds and plan to get more tonight. I'm heading into town tonight to get the stuff for

198

Cloe's Bunny Ranch and to get a long list of supplies I need. I've decided to raise a large garden and raise goats. We will add some cows when we can find them. Several grassy areas would support the cows, but they might make us targets. I'll be glad to help you, but I will demand that you read some books on farming and do your share of the work," Joe said.

"Sounds fair to me. Joe, why don't you and Cobie patch things up? She's as crabby as a mule since you two split up. She's a great woman and not too hard to look at either," Dan said.

"Dan, we were never together. I just helped them out for a while. I'll be honest and tell you that I thought things were going in the right direction, but that woman wants to make it on her own and wants no help from anyone else. She can't stand a helping hand or someone else making a decision. I also think she got jealous when Cloe and I started getting along. I will leave her alone and let her figure her own life out."

"I think she would be worth your effort," Dan said.

"After my last experience, I doubt if any woman is worth the effort," Joe replied. "Which reminds me to try and find a dog, maybe one to breed with Bennie. Although I'd bet, Cobie had him neutered."

"Perhaps you haven't found the right woman," Jane said as she walked up behind Joe.

"I'm not looking for one, and I kind of like it like that for now. Maybe later I'll change my mind," Joe said.

Jane had walked up from behind, laughed, and asked, "Can you put up with one more on your trip into town? We need some supplies also, and I want to go along."

"I'll tell you up front that I don't like the idea, but I've recently learned that people are free to make their own mistakes. If you go, you will do what I say when I say or don't go. If you don't do what I just said, you'll never go with me again," Joe said.

"That sounds familiar. Do what the big man says," Cobie said.

Cloe replied, "Mom that was not fair."

Jane replied, "Joe when I get the experience and courage enough to go by myself, I will. Until then I want your guidance and help. I'm in and won't let you down."

"Okay, get a backpack and a carry bag like mine so we can haul what we find back to the Jeep. I plan to hit the Co-Op and the Grange stores. What do you need?" Joe asked.

"We need canned food, lady's undies, and some chemicals for Cloe so she can tan those Rabbit furs," she said.

That answer made Joe think back to the night he gave Madison the underwear. He got a big grin on his face, and Jane had to say his name several times to get his attention.

"Sorry, I was deep in thought. I'm going to make a quick run back to my cabin and get you another pistol and some ammo. I also have a few of the items on your list," Joe replied.

Jane put her gear together and added several bottles of water, some dried fruit, and a can of Spam to her backpack for the excursion into town. She washed her face and combed her hair in the cabin's bathroom so she wouldn't get catty remarks from Cobie. When she was finished, she had the others gather and asked them to make a list of anything they had to have.

Joe returned as the sun went down and gave Jane a Glock 17, 9mm pistol, and an extra magazine. He then handed her a bag and whispered, "Take these inside and don't let the others see them."

Jane took the bag into her room in the cabin but had to look at the contents. There were several bras and panties in the bag, which confused her greatly. Jane came back outside, and Joe helped her put her backpack on.

They started to leave when Cloe ran up and gave Joe a kiss on the cheek and said, "Joe be careful. I don't want to lose you."

Joe bent down and kissed Cloe on top of the head and said, "Punkin', do what your mom says and don't worry about me. I'm finding that I'm hard to kill and won't get lost. Goodbye."

The two got in the Jeep and went away from the cabin headed away from town then doubled back a mile from the cabin and drove down the hill toward town. They both had to concentrate on the path ahead with the headlights off, so there wasn't much conversation.

Joe stopped at the edge of town behind a building to check his map when Jane asked, "Why did you bring Cobie's underwear to me? That's just mean."

Joe laughed and said, "They weren't Cobie's. She never wore them. The short story is that before I found Cobie and Cloe, I found another woman who moved in with me. She was kidnapped a week later, and I met Cobie when I went to warn

201

them about the kidnappers. Cobie had already killed a couple of those thugs, and she was shot by another. Sorry for the information overload."

"Did you love the woman?"

"I barely knew her, but she was good company," Joe said.

"Good company as in you slept with her," Jane inquired.

"Yes, but I would probably still be trying to run her off between sleeping with her. She was a high maintenance bossy bitch, but she was outstanding in bed. Well, nosey is there anything else you need to know," Joe replied.

"No, but I like to get straight to the point. Joe, I like you, but won't waste my time on you until you get over Cobie," Jane bluntly replied.

"There is no getting over Cobie because we never kissed much less slept together," he replied.

She laughed and said, "Men are so stupid."

He laughed and said, "You sound like Cobie."

Joe saw the two stores were where he remembered just north of East Main on East Hills Road and said, "Jane, we're heading over to the airport and taking the Jeep up the runway until it ends. Then we'll then cut across to East Hills road. The Grange and Co-op stores were just a block up the road. Hey, before I forget, what do you have on your list?"

"I need lady's underwear, some thermal underwear, gloves, and canned vegetables," She answered.

"We should find most of that stuff at the Grange if it hasn't all been looted," Joe replied.

Joe headed north, turned into the airport parking lot, and then drove on to the runway. The evening was clear, but the moon was just peeking above the horizon, so they drove along without worry of being spotted. Joe had to dodge some wreckage from a plane crash but made it safely to the end and then drove to a gate that opened to the main road. He got out of the Jeep with a bolt cutter and cut the lock freeing them to drive on up East Hills Road to the Co-op. He parked behind the building, cut the lock on an overhead door, and drove the Jeep into the building.

Joe looked around the back storage room and found several pallets of animal feed. He placed four fifty pound bags of Rabbit food on the roof of the Jeep, and another four of dog food on the hood then strapped them down. Joe saw several hand pushcarts, gave one to Jane, and told her what to look for to help with the rabbit ranch. They pushed the carts into the main building and began searching for the other items on their lists. The building had been looted of most of the food, guns and, ammo, but most of the rest of the merchandise was left alone.

Joe found the fencing, T posts, and bailing wire in the farming section and then helped Jane find clothing and gloves in the clothing section up front. She found some men's and women's underwear and held up a pair of white large women's underwear.

"Joe, are you fond of Granny Panties? I'll bet you like black thongs better."

Joe saw this coming since he saw Jane earlier that day. She was another Madison and would avoid her in the future.

Of course that didn't stop Joe from checking her out as she held the panties up to her rather shapely body.

He said, "I'll keep that info to myself. Let's find what we need and move on."

"Joe, I was just messing with you," she said but embarrassed that he didn't like her joke.

They brought several carts full of much-needed supplies back to the Jeep, and Joe said, "I know they sell small cargo trailers here. I'm driving around front to get one. I'll be right back."

"Hell no! I'm going with you. Shit man, you have a tendency to lose too many women. I'm stuck like glue to your ass until we get back home."

Joe laughed a deep belly laugh and pointed at the Jeep. They carefully drove around to the front of the building and saw a whole line of trailers chained together. Joe cut the lock, selected a small 5 x 10-foot trailer, and hitched it to the Jeep.

They drove back around to the open door when Jane pointed and said, "Look, something moved by the dumpster. I think it was a woman."

Joe stopped and exited the vehicle with his rifle and walked toward the dumpster. He could smell the body odor before he heard or saw any movement. He said, "Come out and show yourselves. I won't shoot unless you attack us. I won't repeat it before I start shooting. You have three seconds."

"Hold up buddy. We don't want any trouble. We were probably just doing what you are doing. We need food and supplies for our family. Please don't shoot," a man's voice pleaded.

Joe saw a young woman and a man walk to him from behind the dumpster. They were very thin, dirty, and stank of stale beer and sweat. The man had a mouthful of rotten teeth, and his hands were shaking.

"Look, man, all of the food has been stripped from the shelves but look over there in those racks. It won't sound good, but that dog food will keep you alive until you can get some crops in or hunt for food," Joe said.

"I ain't eating no dog food. The government will show up. I just need some real food until they get here. Give us your food; you probably have more than you need," the dirty man said.

Joe didn't see the woman raise the gun until too late. She fired but missed Joe when a shot rang out from behind Joe. Jane shot the woman in the chest, and the man pulled a gun from behind him. This time Joe reacted and shot the man twice in the chest. The noise echoed through the night.

"Jane, let's quickly load what we can because the gang will be here in a few minutes," Joe said as he jumped into the Jeep and drove it into the building.

They threw everything into the trailer and a few things into the back seat before driving away from the building heading north on East Hills Road. There were several cracks from gunfire behind them, but only one bullet struck the Jeep. Joe didn't stop to check the damage and crossed Dead Indian Road to head up into the hills when Joe saw the lights far behind him.

"Jane we have to give these guys the slip, and the going might get rough. I'm going to head up and over the hill in front of us. Then I'll turn back toward town. I will get out with my rifle and let you go on down the hill so I can ambush the men following us. Double back and then come back up between the two hills to our left and wait for me.

Joe got out, and Jane sped on down the hill in the dark. He lay prone on the ground in some bushes and waited for the vehicle to approach. He had to wait for twenty minutes before an old Ford F100 came toward him with a guy on top shining a searchlight into the woods. The truck was going slow and made a great target. Joe shot the man on top then shot the two men in the cab before they could draw their weapons.

He didn't see the man in the back of the truck until it was too late. He saw the flash and hit the ground shooting as he fell. The Mini 14 spat out four shots as Joe fell and the man bled out from two bullets in his legs. Joe lay on the ground with the wind knocked out of him by a bullet that struck the binoculars hanging from his neck. The bullet drove the binoculars into the bottom of his ribs on his left side. A second shot hit the rocky ground and sprayed his legs with bullet fragments and rocks. He struggled for air and couldn't sit up for several minutes.

Joe finally sat up and used his hiking light to check his chest and legs out. The binoculars had saved his life but left him with a huge bruise. He rolled up his pants and saw numerous cuts and holes in his legs. All except two had stopped bleeding, and he held pressure on the last ones until they quit.

He limped to the truck and found three nice Glocks, three AR-15s, and extra magazines for all of the guns. Joe walked over the next hill and down the valley to find Jane and the Jeep. He limped along for half an hour before deciding that he should have walked up the mountain to find her. He rested for a few minutes then continued his trek until he knew he'd gone too far.

Joe noticed that his calves didn't bother him anymore and that he could walk for hours without tiring. If it weren't for the pain from his wound, he would actually enjoy the hike. He knew he had lost a considerable amount of weight, which made walking up and down the mountain trails so much easier. The apocalypse had forced him to exercise and eat less.

Joe's only thought was that she had pulled into a stand of trees and didn't see or hear him walk up the narrow valley. He didn't want to carry the guns any longer and was tired, so he found some dense bushes and found a place to sleep until the sun came up.

Joe didn't sleep much but rested his injured legs until there was enough light to see the tire tracks. His chest still hurt each time he took a deep breath. He crossed the narrow valley and didn't see any tracks, so he started down the valley searching for his Jeeps tracks. He was only a quarter mile from the road at the bottom of the valley when he saw the tire tracks. The tracks headed off into the brush, and he saw the Jeep had cleared a swath of brush through the south side of the valley. He found the Jeep up ahead and was surprised to hear the engine running. He got closer and saw Jane asleep with her head slumped down over the steering wheel.

"Jane. Hey Jane," he called, but she didn't move.

He opened the door, realized that Jane was unconscious, and slumped over the steering wheel with a bloody spot below her shoulder. The bullet had traveled through the back seat, a large box full of seeds, and the front seat before it pierced Jane's jacket and back. She was lucky because the .223 bullet would have ripped a large hole in her chest as it exited if it hadn't been slowed down. Joe took a quick look around him to make sure there was no danger and turned his attention back to Jane.

He lifted her head and checked her chest for an exit wound, but the bullet didn't pass through. He found his First Aid kit, checked her injury, and found there was a bullet fragment lodged about an inch deep against her back upper ribs. He poured alcohol on the hemostat and then the injury to help sterilize them. Jane didn't move as he probed for the jagged bullet fragment until he dislodged it from between two ribs. Joe finished tending to her wound and decided to make her comfortable. He laid the passenger seat back and made Jane as comfortable as possible. He covered her with a blanket and checked to make sure no one was around. Daylight was only a few minutes away, and they were stuck there until dark.

He knew Jane had been lucky the wound stopped bleeding on its own, or she would have bled out and died. He remembered one of the survival manuals mentioned a powder that could be poured on a wound that stopped the bleeding. He would look for a supply of that on his next trip into town.

He heard something move and quickly raised his rifle, but no one was around. He searched the area and saw footprints heading across the hillside. He tracked the person with the intent to kill him slowly for shooting this woman. To his surprise, he came over the top of the hill and saw a body lying in the next valley.

He walked down to the valley and saw the tire tracks of the F100 going right over the dead man. The ones following him had accidentally robbed Joe of the opportunity of killing the man who shot his friend.

He went back to the Jeep and added gas from the Jerry Can to the gas tank. He hoped he was far enough away from the dead men so they wouldn't be found. Joe made himself comfortable so they could hide until the sun went down in nine hours. He couldn't afford anyone following him back to the cabins so he wouldn't travel in the daytime. Jane stirred a couple of times, and he was able to get her to swallow some pain pills and a glass of water. She didn't wake up until late afternoon. Joe spent the day watching for intruders and reading a book on farming that they found at the Co-op. He catnapped a bit but couldn't sleep with the Jeep so far from home.

"What happened? My chest hurts almost as much as my head," Jane said as she opened her eyes and stared at Joe.

"Take it easy and don't move. You were shot in the back below your shoulder. I removed the bullet and stopped the bleeding. I guess you hit your head on the steering wheel when the Jeep stopped against the tree. You'll be okay in a few weeks," Joe said.

"Where are we?

"We're stuck on a hillside a few miles from your cabin. I was afraid to move during daylight for fear of being spotted. We also have to cut south several miles and come in from below the cabin. An experienced tracker could find us in a few hours, but I think these men are just trash from Medford. It will be dark in a few hours, and I'll take you on back to your kids," Joe said.

"Thanks for taking care of me. I really appreciate your help."

"I'm just sorry that I allowed you to go into harm's way. I should have made you stay home," Joe replied.

Jane held back for a minute then said, "Joe your protective streak is adorable, but I'm a grown assed woman and can do what I damn well please. If you hadn't taken me along, I would have gone by myself. Going with you probably saved my life or at least kept me from becoming a gang's love slave."

"Yeah, okay, I'm sorry, but I was raised to be protective of women and children. I don't mean to offend you but only to protect you," Joe said.

"I can see why Cobie is so pissed at you. She's been making a life for the two of them for many years without anyone protecting her, and you come along all macho taking charge. It was a big change that she didn't have time to adjust to," Jane answered.

"So, I just let you make mistakes that get you killed?"

"No, dumbass. You offer training and then act as an equal in a partnership to protect each other. Yes, some women want their big strong man to protect them while they wash clothes and cook supper but most of those women will die off quickly as things get rougher," Jane preached to Joe.

"Sorry for being such an asshole."

"Joe you aren't an asshole. You need to respect that others can contribute and become strong enough to survive," Jane added.

"Well, that was a wakeup call. I'm an asshole and just need to find the local Asshole's Anonymous Meeting to practice the twelve steps to learn how to behave around women. Perhaps they'll have an instruction manual for women that I can use to keep from stepping on my dick all the time," laughed Joe at his own sarcasm.

"Very funny asshole. I thought you might be salvageable, but now I don't know. Besides, if there were a book you men would never read the damned thing," Jane said in frustration.

"Girl, please close your eyes and get some rest before we head back to the cabin," Joe said.

"I got to pee. Help me out of the Jeep."

"Make it fast. I also need to move you to the driver's side," Joe said.

Joe dozed off and slept on and off until midnight. He woke with a start, felt Jane lifting his shirt, and saw her red light shining on his chest.

"I thought you didn't like me and now I find you trying to sneak a feel. Do you want me to flex my chest muscles for you?" Joe asked.

Jane replied, "Again with the smart assed, wise guy routine. I wanted to borrow the field glasses you always have hanging from your neck. When I ran my hand across your chest to find them, you winced in pain. I lifted your shirt and saw a nice black and blue impression of the field glasses on your shirt. What happened?"

"I found the men that were following us, and we traded shots until they were dead and I was on the ground. I thought I was dying for half an hour. I guess I bruised some ribs. I'll be fine in a few weeks," Joe said.

"Everything will be fine in a few weeks. Will those dead men be fine in a few weeks?"

"Nope, I guess they are on their way to hell where I sent them. I say stuff like that, so you won't worry. I guess it's what you call being overprotective," he said.

"Holy crap we just had a breakthrough. That was the first step. You actually admitted that you had a problem," Jane said.

"Now who's being the smart ass," he replied.

The drive back to the cabin was painful but uneventful, as Joe wound his way south then back toward his neighbor's cabin. He stopped a couple of times to make sure no one followed them, which gave them a chance to talk.

"Jane, all kidding aside, I do appreciate you schooling me in how to respect women's abilities and treat them as equals. Hey, isn't that one of the twelve steps?"

"I'm sorry that I was so blunt, but if you want to get back in good with Cobie you need to treat her as an equal and not try to shelter her from life," Jane said.

"Well, like I said, I'm not interested in seeing any woman right now, but the advice you gave me can't hurt," Joe said.

They pulled up between the two cabins and when Joe killed the engine Jane pulled him to her, gave him a kiss, and said, "Joe you might need to be housebroken, but If Cobie doesn't let you catch her you can knock on my door anytime."

He kissed her and said, "I'll keep that in mind, and you can go scavenging with me anytime. I need someone to help watch my back."

Jane patted her side and said, "You can watch my backside anytime."

Joe was very frustrated by Cobie's standoff attitude and Jane was a very attractive woman with a nice backside and a great disposition, yet he didn't want to give up on Cobie yet.

☆

Chapter 15

It was 4:30 am when Joe parked the Jeep by the cabins. He went around to the other side and helped Jane from the Jeep. He picked her up and carried her to the front porch while enduring the pain from his ribs. He didn't see Cobie and Cloe running to them from the other cabin when he heard, "Are you two okay?"

"Jane took a bullet to the back, but she … well let her tell you," Joe said.

"I'll be fine in a few weeks. Joe got to play doctor; he removed the bullet and stopped the bleeding. He is my new hero," Jane said to Cobie.

Cloe bumped into Joe in an attempt to hug him when Jane said, "Be careful Cloe. The big man has some sore ribs."

Joe took Jane up the steps to the front porch as the others came out the door all talking at once. He sat her down in a chair and collapsed on the porch in pain. Cloe helped him to set up and sat down beside him.

Jane's son asked, "Mom, what happened? You were gone two days."

Jane held his hand and said, "We had a few problems but nothing we couldn't handle. Joe and I make a great team, but it appears we have a thing for attracting bullets and bad men."

Ginny and Butch helped Jane to her bed while Cobie and Cloe helped Joe to a chair where Cobie asked, "Joe, what happened? Are you okay?"

"Some meth heads tried to rob us. They shot first, and we got rid of them. When we were about to leave, we saw car lights approaching and headed back here. They shot at us several times. I had Jane drop me off so I could keep her safe and ambush our pursuers. I got them, but Jane was ambushed about a half mile from me. That thug was killed by his own men when they accidentally ran over him in the dark. That's all I got for now. Help me back to the Jeep so I can get some rest," an exhausted Joe said.

"No, I'll get you some blankets and your sleeping bag from the Jeep so you can lie down on the porch."

"Mom let's take him to our cabin," Cloe begged.

"No, he'll be better with the others," Cobie answered.

Cloe fetched the blankets and sleeping bag and set them down beside Joe. She gave him a gentle hug and had tears in her eyes.

"Get some rest, and then we can hear the rest of the story tomorrow," said Cobie as they walked away to their cabin.

"Cobie."

"Yes, Joe."

"I'm sorry for being such a dick head."

Joe watched the two go as he sat on the porch in pain. He tried to get comfortable, but sleep eluded him. He couldn't be mad at Cobie for being independent and cautious about whom she let get close to her because she was just doing exactly what Joe had done. He started to feel lonely and sorry for himself when, like an epiphany, it came to him what he had to do.

Joe struggled to lift his backpack and began the trek to his cabin. He left his portion of the supplies behind and walked as fast as the pain in his ribs would let him.

Dan watched Cobie abandon Joe on the porch and then walk away. He felt that this was a horrible way to treat the man who had helped them so much. He was shocked when Joe rose up and walked into the woods. He wanted to stop Joe and take him into their cabin but knew the man had decided to leave and wouldn't change his mind.

The walk to the cabin was the worst hour of Joe's life. He stumbled in the dark and fell twice tripping over roots. He carefully stepped around his traps and nail boards to enter his cabin. Joe didn't like strong drugs but found the bottle of Lortabs he'd scavenged from town and took two before crashing on the couch. He slept without moving until after dark the next day and only woke up then to use the bathroom. He took two more pills and drank two glasses of water before sleeping for nine more hours.

Joe woke up and walked to the bathroom. He stopped to see himself in the full-length mirror, which was hanging on the bathroom door. He saw a dirty, unshaven man who was thin and hard looking. He had lost forty pounds and gained muscle since he didn't have the junk food, and walked everywhere. He also saw a man who had a new goal in life.

He took a bed sheet from the linen closet, cut it into six-inch wide strips, and used them to bind his chest tight. This helped reduce the pain and made his life bearable for the tasks ahead of him. He cleaned his leg wounds, applied the usual antibiotics, and covered them with bandages.

Joe didn't feel appreciated, or loved by Cobie, so he vowed that morning to get away from Cobie until he could clear his head. He had to get away from her because when she was near, he wanted her and needed her like no woman before. He felt that she acted as though he was only needed to protect her. He decided to use his spare time to sneak into the cities nearby and see if any were still functioning with at least some law and order.

Joe spent the next two weeks recovering from the wound to his leg while thinking about what he wanted from life. He wanted to avoid the others, but Dan or Jane checked on him every other day. He gathered his gear for his trip, checked, and double-checked everything. Joe was ready to go. He left a note on his door that said he would be back in a couple of weeks.

Joe drove the Jeep down the mountain that night. He went around Ashland on backroads and hid the Jeep in a barn between Ashland and Talent on West Jackson Road. He explored the area around him, found a deserted house for his base of operations, and crashed until early evening.

Joe watched the neighborhood from inside the house and only saw a few people venture out during the daytime. He did see several pickups and SUVs with armed men roaming around. Just before dark, he saw three young men with rifles in the ready position walking on Ashland Mine Road. They looked like typical biker trash with their Sons from Hell logos on their back and numerous tattoos. Joe placed his crosshairs on each of them but didn't shoot. He returned to the safety of his hideout and slept most of the day.

He gathered anything of value that he could carry and took it back to the house to be transferred to the Jeep later. Joe mainly searched for medicine, ammunition, and food during his forays. After finding several loads of the necessities, he began searching for luxury and trade items. He knew whiskey, bullets, Viagra and birth control items would be great for trading. He didn't find much but always found something.

Joe left the house a few minutes after midnight and worked his way southwest to Highway 99 and then down that Highway to the Billings Reservoir. He stopped several times along the way to watch the neighborhoods and began noticing which houses and businesses where people still lived. The survivors were being careful to avoid the gangs and thugs prowling the streets. He mainly saw the survivors during early morning hours after most of the gang was sleeping. There were only a few guards awake from about 2 am to midmorning, and the survivors scavenged from around 3 am until daylight.

Initially, Joe found more food and weapons than he could possibly use. After the Jeep was full, he began placing small quantities of food, guns, and ammo in places where the survivors could find them. This became Joe's routine, but soon he found it difficult to find enough to help the people. Joe knew the gangs had gathered most of the items necessary for survival and had discovered where they hid their cache.

It was easy to find the gang's food and supply storage locations because they were always guarded. There would usually be guards at the front of the building with all other doors locked. Joe found a storage site that had been a beauty salon in a strip mall on the north end of town. The guard was posted outside in front of the building. Joe watched the guard for an hour then went behind the building to see how the door was locked.

The doorknob had been destroyed, and the door was secured by a hasp with a standard Master Lock. Joe went to the nearest hardware store, found a similar lock, and took a bolt cutter. He checked on the guard before he cut the lock and entered the building. Food was stacked against the door, so Joe tunneled into the food taking boxes of pasta and canned meat. He filled his carry bag and backpack before placing his duplicate lock on the door.

Joe made several trips to the warehouse that night without being discovered. He dropped most of the food off where he knew the survivors would find it. This kind act made

Joe feel good about himself, and he decided to try harder to help people.

The next night Joe was in the storage building with the door closed. He filled his bags and slowly opened the door with his pistol at the ready. He peeked around the door to make sure the coast was clear and was struck on the head by a hard object.

"The boss ain't going to like this. You fuckin' asshole stole from the gang," the man standing above Joe said.

Joe lay still with his eyes closed but heard, "Damn, I kilt him. The boss don't need to know that I need your pistol and that rifle more than you do. I'ma gonna hide your carcass and take what I need."

The man wrestled with the rifle sling that was trapped by Joe's arm on the ground as Joe slowly drew his knife from its sheath. The man leaned closer to move Joe's arm. Joe brought the blade around and shoved it deep into the man's lower chest while rolling over on top of the man to stifle any scream. The man died silently. Joe locked the door and hid his bags behind a pile of trash before dragging the body to a dumpster two stores down. He struggled to lift the man but finally hefted him over the edge and into the dumpster. Joe closed the door and retrieved his bags before leaving.

The narrow escape scared the crap out of Joe, so he walked carefully back to his hideout and shook as he thought about what had happened. He wanted to help these people, but he didn't want to die to get the job done. He spent the next day working on a better plan that he hoped would keep him safe as he gathered the supplies. He finally came up with a plan to help the survivors help themselves.

Joe followed three men from the city to their basement hideout. Only one of the men had a pistol, but all were very vigilant as they cautiously wound their way back to safety. Joe watched them long enough to know these people could do what he needed so he could free himself from the nightly scavenging.

The men disappeared and then Joe slinked his way through the bushes to just outside the entrance to their hideout. He placed the contents of his bag where they would find the food and left a note, some locks and keys, and the bolt cutter. The letter gave the survivors instructions on how to pilfer from the gangs without being caught. He always signed the notes with "Joe" in small letters. Joe was pleased with his accomplishment and left for his hideout.

Joe left the same care package and note for several groups the next day then he loaded everything into his Jeep after midnight and drove to the south side of Medford. He drove around the towns by heading up into the hills and taking back roads to avoid being spotted by the gangs. Joe remembered that Medford had a National Guard Armory and he wanted to find some military rifles. He hid the Jeep in an industrial complex several blocks from the armory.

He slept until midnight and had a breakfast of jerky and peanut butter. He missed the good old country breakfasts his mom used to prepare for him and his dad on the weekends, as he stuffed his mouth with jerky. He liked jerky and peanut butter but not for breakfast. He could remember the smell of strong black coffee waking him up on Sunday morning and the smell of bacon frying. Just thinking about those days made his mouth water. He swore to himself that he would find some chickens, pigs, and a way to make bread so he could have a proper breakfast in spite of the apocalypse.

Joe crept around the Walmart building to see that the Armory was guarded by two gang members with AR-15s. He walked back around the Walmart to approach the armory from behind and found himself in the fenced in NG vehicle staging area. There were signs that a major fight had occurred around the trucks. Joe saw hundreds of bullet holes in the trucks and shell casings on the ground. He searched around on the ground with his penlight and saw where pools of blood had dried.

Joe began searching the trucks and found some useful equipment and several flashlights. He saw a line of large trucks and broke into the end truck, which was full of construction tools. He moved on to the next and found what he was looking for. The truck had several locked metal containers that only took Joe a minute to open with his pry bar and bolt cutters. One had metal ammunition boxes, and the other had metal cases with scopes, red dot sights, and walkie-talkies.

Joe took several cases of each of the items and made two trips back to the Jeep before he began his search again. He walked along the line of trucks and noticed a foul odor coming from one of the trucks. He lifted the tarp on one of the trucks and was frightened when he saw three dead soldiers. The men were riddled with bullet holes. They had died fighting with their rifles and pistols in their hands. Joe found several M4s along with a dozen M19 Berretta 9 mm pistols.

Joe slung the M4s across his shoulders after stuffing six of the Berettas in his backpack and was able to make it safely back to his Jeep before daylight. Joe then rearranged his load to make room for the weapons and gear by securing cases of food and cloth bags of food to the roof and hood of the Jeep.

Joe was now mentally ready to go home but wanted to make one last trip to the Armory to fetch more ammo. He double-checked the Jeep to make sure it was ready to head home as soon as he returned from the armory.

Joe strapped his pistol belt to his waist and put on one of the tactical vests. He placed a Beretta in his side holster and another in the vest holster. He wanted to have weapons that used the same magazines. He then filled the ammo pouches with four spare M4 and four 9mm magazines. He then slung his carry bag's sling over his shoulder and selected one of the M4's to go with him. He checked his equipment and left for the armory.

The walk to the armory was uneventful, but he began to see more gang activity than usual as he approached the Walmart building. He went on around the backside of the store only to find a flurry of activity at the back of the building. Four of the massive military trucks were lined up behind the Armory, and there were dozens of people unloading food and other supplies from the trucks and taking the cases through the overhead door to the armory. The trucks were only ten yards from Joe's supply of ammunition in the line of trucks.

Joe watched and about the time he thought they would be done, another convoy of trucks rolled up to be unloaded. Joe decided to go back to his Jeep and make tracks back to his cabin. He snuck along the walls of the Walmart in the dark to get back to the Jeep. He walked past a dumpster when abruptly two men sprang from the shadows and tried to rob him.

The men were dirty and reeked of alcohol. They had machetes in their hands, and one said, "Mac, just give us your guns and we'll let you walk away. You shoot us, and the whole damned gang will kill all three of us."

"Why should I believe you will let me live," Joe said as he drew his pistol and pointed it at the men.

"Because you don't have a choice."

Joe looked at the men in the dim light, and he could see the open sores, and rotted teeth that mark the long-term for meth and drug users. He was surprised that they had stayed alive so long. Then he thought, *cockroaches would outlive all of us.* The men stank of body odor and piss, which made Joe sick to his stomach.

"You always have a choice," Joe said as he shot both men in the chest.

Joe quickly placed the gun in one of the men's hand and stuck the other's machete deep into the other man's wound. He threw down his emergency rations, a flashlight, and two magazines for the Beretta. He ran across the parking lot and hid in a car to watch.

A few minutes later, half a dozen men came slowly around the corner with rifles ready. They carefully advanced to the dumpster when one of the men saw the bodies. The men took the guns and other items and went back to the armory. Apparently, they bought Joe's staged robbery.

Joe was now ready to go home. He drove the Jeep slowly through the mountain roads until he camped for the night south of Ashland to spend the daylight hours. The next night he left Ashland after midnight. He drove further south and approached the cabins from the southwest. He parked short of Dan's cabin and waited for dawn. He was damned happy to see the cabins and couldn't wait to see his friends.

☆

Chapter 16

Joe sat in the Jeep reading one of his Grandma's letters before greeting his friends.

Dear Joe:

I hope this letter finds you in good health and ready for an early spring. Anyway, I hope spring is early this year because I hate long hard winters. I do hope you plant a large garden in the clearing by the cabin and grow fresh vegetables.

Have you found a girlfriend yet? A young man needs a woman in his life, and a strong-willed woman would do you good. She also needs a strong back to live in the woods, but most men are more interested in girls other assets.

As I ramble on, I hope you start the treasure hunt after you get your spring chores completed. I assure you that it will be fun if you can bear to find the treasure map and don't cave into complacency.

Gotta go.

Love Grandma.

Joe wondered *what the hell his Grandma meant by the treasure and treasure maps.* Joe was deep in thought when he heard Dan yell, "Who's there?"

"Joe is back. Tell everyone Joe is back," Dan yelled.

A sleepy boy answered, "But dad it's only five o'clock, and everyone is asleep."

Several people ran out of the cabin and swarmed Joe as he stepped out of the Jeep. Jane was leading the charge to the truck.

"Joe are you okay? You've been gone over two weeks, and we started wondering if you would ever come back to us," Jane said.

"Well, I'm here and plan to stay here a long while. There is nothing in town for me, and I missed my cabin and my friends," Joe responded.

Joe saw Cobie and Cloe walking from the cabin heading in his direction. He ran to Cloe, picked her up, and swung her around as he said, "Cloe, I missed you girl. How is the Bunny Ranch doing?"

Cloe hung on Joe's neck hugging him for a minute and said, "I was afraid you weren't coming back. I missed you so much."

"Cloe, I will always come back to you, and you can always count on me when you need it," Joe said between hugs.

"Joe, tell us about..." Jane started to say when Cloe interrupted.

"Joe, come see my rabbits. We already have a bunch of babies," Cloe said as she pulled him away from the others.

Joe said, "I'll be back in a little while after my girl shows me the rabbits."

Cobie walked along with her daughter and Joe to the rabbit pen beside their cabin. Cloe and the boys had built a nice rabbit house that was filled with dried grass. The pen was twenty feet by twenty and was made with T posts and chicken wire.

Joe looked at it and said," Are you losing any rabbits to the hawks and owls?"

"Oh no, two disappeared this week. I thought they ran off," Cloe said.

"The pen needs a roof to keep the birds from swooping down and dining on your rabbits," Joe replied.

Cobie interrupted the conversation and asked, "Joe have you had breakfast?"

Joe turned to her and said, "I thought you were still mad at me, so I don't want to bother you."

"Joe I want you to come eat breakfast with us this morning then we can all go down to Dan's and let you fill them in on your exploits. Besides, you apologized for being a dick head. Please eat with us," Cobie said.

"I would love to have breakfast with you, but let me get a few things from my Jeep first. I have some surprises," Joe replied.

Joe walked down to the Jeep and told the others that he would be back down to fill them in on his trip after breakfast with Cobie and Cloe.

"Hey, I have some supplies for you," Joe said as he took several cases of food from the back of the Jeep and handed them to Dan.

Joe drove the Jeep over to Cobie's cabin and parked by the rabbit pen. He took several cases of food from the Jeep into the cabin after taking his boots off. He took several packages from one of the boxes and gave them to Cobie.

"Cobie, these are packages of freeze-dried scrambled eggs for campers. Could you ..." Joe said before Cobie gave him a big hug.

"Joe, I'd kill for some scrambled eggs. You are my hero. I'll fix some to go with our fried rabbit."

Joe took a can from the box, walked up behind Cobie, and said, "What would you do for some coffee?"

"I'd give a man a kiss for a good cup of coffee," she said as she leaned into Joe and kissed him on the cheek and then whispered, "Joe, please stay with us for a while. Cloe needs you."

Joe looked to see that Cloe had gone outside and said, "What about Cloe's mom?"

"What about Cloe's mom?" Cobie replied.

"Does Cloe's mom miss me and want me around?"

"Cloe's mom missed you even though you are the most frustrating man I have ever met. I do appreciate your apology you gave me when you left. I know I can also be difficult so I apologize for that. Let's start over. Please stay with us," Cobie said.

Joe pulled her to his chest and asked, "What will we be starting? I don't want to misunderstand your meaning. I'm thinking about kissing you."

Cobie felt wonderful in his arms but pulled away as she replied, "Joe I want to be your friend. I don't know if I have more to offer right now. If you need a girlfriend, you might want to go down to the other cabin. Jane could be another Madison for you."

"Cobie, let's be friends and then worry about the other stuff later. You hate men, and I had a bad time with my fiancee, so I'm good with us being friends, for now. I missed you a lot and really missed talking with you," Joe said.

"I missed your friendship and watching how you were so good to my daughter," Cobie said.

"You are a strong woman but you don't try to manipulate me, and you are always honest. I need that out of you. I will try not to be bossy and let you do your thing without trying to be too protective," Joe said.

Cobie looked at him and replied, "Thanks for realizing that I need to be my own person. Now let's cook some eggs, dick head."

"So is that a promotion or demotion to the dick head status?"

"Promotion," Cobie said as she laughed on the way to the kitchen.

Cloe had been standing just inside the door listening and said, "Joe, I don't care what she calls you as long as she's smiling and we are all back together. Let's talk bunnies after breakfast."

The eggs were powdered but were like a gourmet meal to the three who hadn't seen a normal breakfast in months. The eggs tasted good but had a green tint to them and were a bit rubbery. They ate every morsel and then asked Cobie to prepare another batch. They laughed and joked around the table until Cloe asked him about his trip into the city.

"I spent most of the time resting during daytime hours and scavenging for food and supplies during the nights. I was able to gather a Jeep full of food, weapons, and other supplies," Joe said.

"Are there many survivors?" Cloe asked.

"Yes, there are people all over the city hidden in basements and homes that are scared of the gangs. There are dozens of gang members that have taken charge of the city and kill anyone who doesn't do what they are told. The crime is horrible. The captured survivors are slaves," Joe said.

"Cloe, go outside and get your chores done so we can head down to the neighbors after Joe and I do the dishes," Cobie said.

Cloe put on her boots, pistol belt, and coat before heading outside. Her mom watched her strap the 9mm to her hip and wondered if kids would ever be kids again. She was afraid they would become hardened to this new life as kids on the American frontier were back in the 1850s.

Joe gathered the plates and took them to the sink to help Cobie when Cobie said, "Joe I was just kidding about you helping me."

"Cobie, we are in a new world where you will be helping me plow the ground, fight gangs, and well, just survive. The least I can do is help wash dishes and carry my own weight around the house. I don't think there is a man or woman's work anymore. We all work and do the best we can. Of course, there will be work that I can't do, or you can't do, but we'll figure that out as time goes by," Joe said as he watched Cobie's expression.

"Joe, I totally agree. I do need you to teach me what you know about guns, traps, and any other survival skills. I also want one of those military-style weapons," Cobie said but wondered how Joe would react.

"I had already planned on the training and have a couple of surprises for you. I brought back several toys to share with you and Cloe. I have an extra AR-15 for you and Cloe, and I'll give Dan my Mini 14. I now have several ARs and a few M4s plus several more 9mm pistols and a bunch of ammunition. We need to share with the neighbors, but our first concern is to protect ourselves," Joe replied.

Cobie looked concerned and said, "My first reaction was that we are selfish, but now I know that you are right. My first concern is for Cloe's safety then our's before the others. Share what you can with them, and we'll keep the rest and hide any weapons we don't use right away. Oh, I forgot to tell you that Dan was once a policeman in his home city. He can help with the training."

"So I'm a dick head but worth saving."

"You'll have to do until something better comes along," Cobie pinched his side and laughed.

Joe didn't even mention that what she said goes both ways since Cobie was in a good and playful mood. He cut his losses and said, "Cobie, my cabin is much larger and better equipped than this one. I have electricity and running water. I even have a hot water heater that works. I want you to move in with me. It would mean less firewood to cut and would save me travel time. I have two large bedrooms, you and Cloe can have one, and I'll take the other. I'm not hitting on you just trying to be practical."

"Oh, my God, we could take regular baths. I've been afraid that my smell would run you off," Cobie said.

Joe pulled her close, moved his face close to hers, and breathed deeply. He then said, "You smell pretty good to me. So, what do you think?"

"I agree on moving into your home. I'll ask Cloe, and if she agrees, we'll move. Oh, you'll have to build another Bunny Ranch at your cabin. You know that Cloe loves you and really missed you while you were gone," Cobie said.

"I missed both of you and thought a lot about you while I was gone. Cobie, promise me that If I do or say anything stupid that you will let me know. Don't hold back," Joe said.

She patted him on the back and said, "There's hope for you yet."

Cobie thought for a moment and asked, "Joe why did you go on the trip to town? It was very dangerous, and you could have been killed."

"Hon, when I left, I really didn't care about living or dying. You hated me. I lost Madison. Damn, I just felt powerless and wanted to take charge of my life. I ended up helping a bunch of survivors by teaching them how to steal food from the gangs."

"What about Jane? She was worried sick about you and cares for you," Cobie said as her voice trembled.

"Jane is a great woman but not the one I want," Joe answered.

Cobie changed the subject and asked, "Did you kill enough men to make you feel better?"

"No, I only fought to protect myself. There are many thugs that need to be killed, but it was time to come home to you and Cloe. I was mad at you when I left but couldn't hold it against her."

"Are you still mad at me?"

"I was for a while but couldn't get my mind off you and my little Munchkin. Cobie I love you," Joe said.

She pushed him away and said, "Later. We'll discuss that when we get back."

They put their coats on, grabbed their rifles, and went outside. The sun felt good on their faces and warmed the morning up to moderate spring temperature. The day would warm up to the low fifties by midafternoon. They walked over to the Bunny Ranch where Cloe had a large rabbit in her lap. It was an expectant mother rabbit, and Cloe was petting and talking to it.

"Honey, what would you think about moving into Joe's cabin? It's much larger and has several advantages over this one?" Cobie asked.

Cloe looked at her mom, and Joe then looked at her rabbit pen and said, "I like the idea, but we have to move my rabbits and the rabbit pen."

Joe replied, "I'll build you another pen before we move and if you're okay with it, we'll leave a few rabbits for the neighbors."

"That works for me," Cloe said as she rose to her feet and hugged Joe.

"Put the rabbit away, and we'll join the others so Joe can tell them about his trip. Get your rifle, and we'll head out," Cobie said.

Joe opened the passenger side door and brought out two AR-15s and six extra loaded magazines. He also retrieved two tactical vests that had a holster for their Glocks. The vests had numerous pockets for the rifle and pistol magazines. He handed them to the girls and said, "Please take these. This will give you much more firepower. I'll give the Mini 14 to Dan along with some of the other weapons. I want my wo... err...you two gals to be prepared to fight if necessary."

Both weapons were Springfield M&P15s with tactical stocks, red dot sights, and a one-point sling. Joe demonstrated how to load, aim, and fire the rifles and then showed them how to load the magazines.

"Joe, I thought all electronics got fried by those EMP bombs," Cloe said.

"I guess these were stored in metal foil bags inside of fully enclosed metal gun safes. The gangs must have stolen them from a gun shop or serious collector. They were shielded from the EMP waves. The four power sights take a bit of getting used to but are perfect for up close and medium range targets," Joe replied.

Joe gave them an AR, a 9mm pistol, and spare loaded mags, while he took the M4 and 9mm Beretta. The extra weapons would go to Dan and his crew. He slung a bag filled with additional boxes of .223 rounds over his shoulder, and they left to visit the neighbors.

Joe saw Butch first and waved at the boy as they approached the neighbor's cabin. Butch ran up to meet them with his shotgun cradled in his arms. He stopped beside Cloe and said, "Hello Cloe. Are you going to be here for a while? I have guard duty for the next hour and don't want to miss you."

Cobie replied, "Don't worry Butch. We'll be here for a couple of hours. Cloe, why don't you hand us the extra guns and keep Butch company while we visit with the others."

"Mom, I'd like that. Butch and I are planning how to breed hybrid rabbits and get more meat from them," Cloe said.

They walked away with Joe laughing and Cobie punching him in the side.

Joe said, "I'll bet your heart skipped a beat when she said, "Butch and I are planning how to breed." If she had stopped at the word breed, you would have shot the poor boy."

"Joe, that wasn't funny. I don't want her growing up too fast, even though I know she has to. I don't want to think about her in that way," Cobie said.

"I'm sorry, but it's not what you think. It's what those two think, and that boy is sweet on Cloe," Joe said, and then added, "I'm sorry. That was probably the type of comment that gets me in trouble."

Cobie pulled Joe close to her and kissed him on the lips before she said, "I was kidding you, but we do need to watch them."

Joe saw Jane and Dan approaching and knew the kiss was Cobie marking her territory in front of the competition. He replied, "Darling, I will always watch over Cloe and you. I'll try not to stifle you, but I won't let anyone hurt you. You can kiss me anytime."

"Hey, Dan! Hey Jane! I brought Joe down for a visit, and we are bearing gifts," Cobie said as she handed Jane a rifle and the pistol.

"It's great to see you Joe and thanks for the gifts. Let's sit out on the porch in the sun and enjoy this spring weather," Dan said.

Jane walked up to Joe, gave him a hug, and then went into the house to get some more chairs. She watched Cobie sit down close to Joe. That was all Jane needed to know about her chances with Joe. She had the kids bring all the kitchen chairs out to the porch, and they sat there listening to Joe tell them about his adventures.

Joe gave them the same high-level overview of his exploits that he gave Cobie and Cloe that morning. He then whispered to Dan that he should send the kids away and they waited until the kids were out of range. The kids left the porch, and Joe told them his story in detail. They were amazed that he was able to help so many people and return home safely.

Ginny was shocked that Joe had to kill several men even though they were trying to harm him. She said, "It's a shame that we can't put those men in prisons instead of having to kill them."

Joe didn't know how to answer that absurd statement, so he kept quiet and listened.

"Dan, Joe, and I discussed this situation this morning. We all need you and Joe to teach us what you know about weapons and tactics to help us protect our people. We must eliminate threats before they attack us. Ginny, Jane, we also need to train all of the children how to protect themselves and how to fight if attacked. We are no different than the people who settled the old west. They were under constant threat of attack by the Indians, and we will have similar threats," Cobie said with a conviction in her voice.

Ginny started crying and sobbed as she said, "I can't let my babies shoot people and get shot at."

Dan held her and gave Cobie a thumbs up sign. Jane stood up to stretch and said, "My boys and I will be ready for training when you guys are ready to train us."

Joe said, "I'll help where I can, but I think Dan has much more knowledge than I do. Dan?"

"Joe, I can teach them a lot about weapons, proper shooting techniques, and how to defend themselves in hand to hand fights, but you will have to teach all of us how to kill people. I was on the force 11 years and never shot anyone. I know I can if I have to save my wife and kids but never have had to go that far," Dan said.

Joe answered, "The best thing we can do is to stay in these woods and not draw outside attention to ourselves. I took several of my Grandpa's books with me to read last month and learned that most people will die off in the first three to six months. The problem is that the criminals were already organized into gangs. They might survive by preying on the good people who don't have guns and don't know how to fight. We must avoid contact as much as possible until we can defend ourselves."

☆

Chapter 17

Cloe was very impressed with the electric lights at Joe's cabin. She was familiar with solar power but had never seen it in use before. Cobie was floored by the running water, and the propane fired water heater.

"Joe does the water heater work," Cobie asked.

"Yes, I tested it once, but I use the wood stove to heat my water. We can use it to heat bath water but not every time we heat water, or we'll run out of propane," Joe said.

Joe loaded the old truck with as much of Cobie and Cloe's possessions as he could. He wanted to make a few trips to his cabin as possible to avoid making ruts on the forest floor. The ruts could lead outsiders to the cabin. Joe made three trips and took a different route each time. In a few weeks, the grass would be green and grow waist high hiding the tracks.

On the third day, they moved the last of their loads and told the neighbors, they were done with the cabin. Jane had expressed her intention to relocate to the old cabin. This would make more room for Dan's family but would still keep them close together for mutual defense.

The move completed Cobie began rearranging the cabin to suit herself. Joe moved furniture and tried to assist as much as possible. Cobie avoided discussing their budding relationship but did sit on the couch with Joe's arm around her while they relaxed before bed. On a few occasions, she laid her head on his lap as she read one of the survival manuals. Joe began to wonder if Cobie would ever commit to a meaningful relationship.

Spring had begun, the days were warmer, and the sun rose earlier each day. The mountains of Oregon were beautiful year round, but the springtime is especially enjoyable with the valleys turning green and the plants and trees putting out buds and later flowers. The sunshine was a welcome part of their day as it warmed their faces and arms. Joe had the girls join him at noon every day in a short sunbathing ritual that increased their morale. On a few occasions, they all wore shorts and t-shirts during their sunbathing.

Dan and Joe took two hours every day after lunch to teach the others about their weapons and how to use them effectively. Joe shared his stock of pellet rifles so they could demonstrate proper shooting techniques. The live but silent shooting exercises significantly increased everyone's accuracy.

Joe taught everyone the art of fighting with a knife after he read every article on the subject from his Grandpa's books. He made the books available to everyone. They all worked hard to become proficient enough on several survival topics so they could teach the others.

Joe watched Cobie and Jane wrestling on the ground after Dan taught them how to fight. Cloe laughed as her mom pinned Jane to the ground for a minute before Jane looped a leg around Cobie and pitched her to the ground. Joe pulled for Cobie to Jane's dismay, but his support made Cobie's day.

"Ladies, that was excellent. Tomorrow you will learn how to disable a larger attacker. Joe and I are trying to manufacture some ...err...cups to protect the family jewels from your vicious assaults."

"Yes, girls, I want my hubby's jewels intact after we beat up on them tomorrow," Ginny laughed as she spoke.

"Mom, that's too much information," her daughter Dot exclaimed.

Joe took a towel and a bottle of water over to Cobie who was exhausted from the training. She took a drink and poured the rest of the water on her head. Joe sopped the water from her hair with a towel and tried to dry it.

"Joe, I'll look like a weightlifter when we get through with the training. My muscles are so sore," Cobie said.

"I have a jar of Blue Emu back at the cabin you can rub on your muscles," Joe said.

"Could you do it for me? I'm so tired, I could fall asleep right now," Cobie replied.

"Well, we need to get on back to the cabin. Cloe grab your gear. I'll get mine and your moms."

Cobie asked Joe to haul water to the big tub so she could take a bath and Joe answered, "Let me turn the hot water heater on and the tub will fill itself with nice hot water."

She lay on the couch and asked Joe to hang the sheet up that hid the tub from the rest of the cabin. After the water was hot, Joe filled the tub to about five inches deep. The water was hot but perfect to sooth Cobie's sore muscles. She walked behind the sheet and began to take her clothes off.

"Cloe, go out and tend to your rabbits," Cobie said.

"Okay mom, I'll be outside until super," Cloe said as she left the cabin.

"I'll go out and join Cloe with the rabbits so you can bathe in private," Joe said.

"Please stay and keep me company. I'm behind a sheet, and you can't see anything. Stay and talk to me, please Joe," Cobie begged.

"I don't want you to think I would take advantage of our arrangement," Joe replied.

Cobie stuck her head around the sheet and said, "Joe come here."

Joe walked over to her, and she reached around with one arm and drew him close to her. She kissed him long and hard, and then said, "I'm so glad you came back. I think I know how to keep you here with us."

"If that was a sample of things to come; I'm in," Joe replied.

"Joe, Jane is so jealous that you're living with us. She tried to kill me this afternoon," Cobie smiled to herself as she washed.

"Yes, she is jealous. During our trip back from town, she told me that if you didn't want me that her door would always be open," Joe replied.

"Joe do you want to go to her door?" Cobie said as she toyed with Joe.

"I don' know how to answer that. I have this other woman who kinda likes me every now and then but not enough to commit. I care for her a lot, and I'm waiting for her to make up her mind," Joe said.

"I hear she is warming up to you and rubbing that sore muscle stuff all over her body might seal the deal," Cobie said as she stood up and dried off.

Cobie walked out from behind the curtain with only a towel on, walked over to Joe, and kissed him. She then lay down with her back up on the couch. She pulled the towel down until it only covered her butt and said, "Rub that stuff on my legs first, then my arms, and then my back."

Joe began rubbing the cream onto her legs and then said, "Darn Cloe might come in. This wouldn't look good."

"I told Cloe to give us a couple of hours of privacy to discuss a few things. Get back to rubbing my back that feels so good. I'm pretty sure that after tonight there won't be any going to Jane's door," Cobie moaned.

Joe finished her backside, and she said," That was damned good. Turn your head so I can roll over."

He turned around until she said to begin rubbing again. When he turned, she had placed the towel over her waist, and a washcloth covered her breasts. Cobie looked up at him and said, "Rub that stuff on every bit of skin you can see. Don't touch any other parts. I think your girl is warming up to you but really wants the rubdown before she makes up her mind."

Joe rubbed the cream on her arms legs and upper chest before moving to her stomach. He rubbed her in a very sensuous way until he said, "You know that you are killing me."

"I know, and it is so much fun watching you squirm. I think your girl has made up her mind. Lock the door and take your clothes off," Cobie said.

She threw the towel to the floor and then drew him close and kissed him long and hard. Joe locked the door and scrambled to take his pants off. They lay down on the couch when suddenly Bennie began growling and barking outside. Then they heard Cloe screaming, "Help me."

Joe put his pants on, grabbed his rifle, and ran out the door. He saw Cloe on top of the truck swinging a stick at a mountain lion that was trying to attack her. The lion jumped onto the hood of the truck and crouched to spring at Cloe. There was another that had Bennie cornered against the porch. Joe aimed and fired at the one trying to attack Cloe. He shot twice, and the beast fell to the ground. He turned to shoot the other lion and saw it running off into the woods with Bennie chasing it. He shot the first lion twice more to make sure it was dead.

Joe went to Cloe who was down on her knees crying. He picked her up off the truck's fender and carried her to the house. Cobie came running out of the house half dressed and met them on the porch.

"Baby, are you okay. What happened?" Cobie asked.

"A huge cat tried to eat Bennie, and I hit it with a big stick. I forgot to take my gun out with me. Please save my dog," Cloe sobbed.

Cobie held her daughter on the couch and asked, "Joe what do we do? I want to save Bennie, but we don't want to get anyone else hurt."

"Darling, I'll track Bennie and bring him back. He's probably got the cat stuck in the top of a tree by now and is too stubborn to come home until he catches the cat. I'll be back in a few hours," Joe said.

Joe finished dressing and took his gear and rifle to the door. He turned as he saw Cobie coming over to him. She said, "Be careful and don't get hurt."

He left the cabin and found tracks leading north toward the top of the ridge where the old Forest Service road ran across the top of his property. A few minutes later, the tracks headed due east along the ridge. After half an hour, he heard Bennie howling and knew he was close.

***

"Baby girl, I need to go help Joe. Lock the door and keep your rifle beside you. Joe and I just made up, and I'm not about to lose him to some dumb assed lion," Cobie said.

"Mom, my guess is your discussion with Joe went very well since you both ran out of the cabin half dressed. Please bring Joe back. He is more important than Bennie. Be careful," Cloe said.

Cobie put her hiking clothes on and shouldered her backpack. She strapped her Glock to her hip and slung her AR-15 over her shoulder before waving bye to Cloe. She began following the tracks but missed seeing them turn east and kept going north. She burst out of the woods onto the Forest Service road and didn't see the two old trucks heading east.

She was in such a hurry that she slipped on wet leaves and stumbled out in front of the lead vehicle. The driver saw her at the last second and slammed on the brakes. The vehicle came to a stop but not before hitting Cobie. Her rifle flew through the air and landed in the woods. Her body was thrown clear of the truck and struck the ground violently. She lay there as blood flowed from a gash on the side of her head leaving her unconscious.

"John, you hit that man. We need to check on him," Gail said.

"There might be others. It could be a trap," John replied.

"I'll watch the woods with my gun ready. Please check on the man," Gail replied.

A man and a woman came running up from the trail vehicle and asked, "What happened? Did you hit something?"

"Hey Gail, come here. It's a young woman, and she's barely alive," John replied.

"Pick her up and put her in the back of the truck. I'll tend to her so we can get back on the road. She can join us. The poor thing looks like she's had it rough living in the woods alone," Gail said.

A third man came from the other truck and helped place Cobie in the back of Gail's truck. He looked at Cobie and said, "She sure is a pretty young thing. Gail, tend to her. We've got another ten miles to go before it gets too dark to travel."

***

Joe shot the lion and left it at the base of the tree where it fell. He planned to come back and skin it the next day. He grabbed Bennie by the collar and forced the dog to go with him as they walked back toward the cabin. Joe heard a noise coming from the direction of the Forest Service road and ducked down into a crouch behind a tree. He looked in the direction of the sound and saw two trucks speeding east. He stayed hidden until they were long gone.

It took a lot of effort, but he was finally able to drag Bennie back to the cabin and knocked on the door. Cloe came out, hugged Bennie, and smothered Joe with kisses.

"Joe thanks so much for saving my dog. I love you, Joe. Hey, where is my mom?"

"What do you mean? Your mom is here with you."

"Joe, mom took off after you. Oh no! Go get my momma," Cloe said as she broke down into sobs.

"Cloe, this is important. Do not follow me or leave the cabin. I will bring your mom back in a few hours. Stay in the cabin. If for some reason it takes me longer than I think it will, go to Dan and stay with them until we get back."

Joe left the cabin and tracked Cobie's footprints to the road. He saw the fresh tire tracks and followed them east for a few yards until he saw numerous footprints. The sun was going down as he found the pool of blood in the gravel.

He fell to his knees crying because Cobie's tracks ended in the mass of footprints beside the pool of blood. Joe cried for several minutes as he tried to clear his head. He had to find Cobie. He knew she had to be alive or he would have found her body. He searched the entire area and found her rifle in the weeds just inside the forest. The stock was bent, and the handguard was shattered. He also saw where the gravel had been pushed as the trucks braked hard just a few yards from the pool of blood.

Joe now knew that Cobie had been run over by the lead truck and taken by the people in those trucks. His mind raced through the possible things that could have happened and couldn't come up with a good one. The best he could pray for was that the truck accidentally hit Cobie, that the people took her with them, and were caring for her. Joe would not admit to himself that Cobie was gone and chances were that he would never see her again.

Joe followed the trail using his flashlight until he lost the tracks several miles from where he found the blood on the road. The road split in two, and it was too dark to see the tracks. He wanted to pursue the trucks until he found Cobie

249

but knew he couldn't find the tracks in the dark and Cobie would want him to go back to Cloe and make sure that she was safe. It was now five hours since he had left Cloe, and he stopped by the cabin for some water before going to Dan's to get her. He opened the door to find a rifle pointed at his chest and a frightened girl.

"Where's my mom. You said that you would bring her back," Cloe asked.

Joe had thought about what to tell Cloe on the way back from his search. He didn't want to mention the blood and the accident. He said, "Cloe, your mom has been kidnapped, and I'm going to find her and bring her back."

"Who took my mom? I'll kill those bastards," Cloe said between sobs.

"Darling, I don't know, but I will find her. I promise," Joe replied.

"Why would they take my mom? Was it those Islamic terrorists?" Cloe asked.

"I don't think so. The tire tracks were from a pickup. The terrorists drove military-style vehicles," Joe said.

"What do we do now, Joe?" she asked.

"I need you to stay with Dan and Ginny while I search for your mom. I can travel faster by myself," Joe said.

"I won't go, and if you make me, I will follow you after you leave. I have shot men that tried to hurt my mom before, and I can do it again. Take me with you," Cloe pleaded.

"Damn, you are hardheaded enough to do just that. Okay, we get some rest and head out in the morning. We will tell the others what happened and ask them to watch over my cabin. Cloe, this won't be easy. We will plan a two-week trip to be on the safe side. We'll take Bennie with us to help pack some gear and to be our watchdog at night. Now get to bed so we can get up early," Joe said.

Joe lay in his bed thinking about how unfair life had been to him when he said to himself, "Grandma, I need to read a letter that tells me how to save the woman I love."

His mind heard," Joe, go *find your woman and kill the assholes that took her. Get off your ass and get moving before it's too late.*"

"Yes Grandma," Joe replied.

Joe fell asleep thinking that he was crazy for talking to a dead woman. The next morning Joe gathered supplies while Cloe slept a while longer. It took another couple of hours for them to leave on their quest.

Joe looked back at the cabin and wondered if they would ever return. He looked at Cloe and said, "We're burning daylight. Let's go find your mom and my best friend."

Cloe took his hand and said, "Joe, I'm not coming back without my momma."

The End

***American Apocalypse: Book II-
Descent Into Darkness should be
published by February 2018.***

*Thanks for reading my novel and please don't
forget to give it a great review on Amazon.
Remember to read my other books on
Amazon.*

AJ Newman

Remember to push the **Follow** button below
the author's photo on Amazon to follow AJ
Newman and get notice of new books.

All novels contain some errors. If you find an
error, please send a note with the error to the
author at ajnewman123@yahoo.com

If you like my novel, please post a review on Amazon.

To contact or follow the Author, please leave
comments @:

To view other books by AJ Newman, go to Amazon to my Author's page:

http://www.amazon.com/-/e/B00HT84V6U

A list of my other books follows.

Thanks,   AJ. Newman

☆

Please read my friend, Mack Norman's novel "Rogues Origin."
I highly recommend the series, "Rogues Apocalypse.

Rogues Origin tells the story of how some unique people survive and
prosper during an apocalypse caused by a nuclear EMP attack on the USA
and the rest of the world. These people are unique because they quickly
decide to do what it takes to survive before everything falls entirely apart.
The main characters are a Post-Apocalyptic Science Fiction writer, a
crooked Federal Marshal, an NYPD Policeman, a Mobster, and a woman
who is a mob enforcer.

What would you do if you knew you had a few hours before the shit hit the
fan. These people take action and fight back against the apocalypse.

BOOKS BY
AJ NEWMAN
&
MACK NORMAN

Rogues Apocalypse Series:
Rogues Origin
Rogues Rising
Rogues Journey

AJs and Mack's books are available on Amazon @

https://www.amazon.com/Mack-
Norman/e/B0779JZWC4/ref=dp_byline_cont_ebooks_1

-

Books by my good friend Cliff Deane

BOOKS BY CLIFF DEANE
Vigilante Series
Into The Darkness
Into the Fray
Pale Horse
No Quarter
The Way West
Indian Territory

Cliff's books are available on Amazon @

https://www.amazon.com/Cliff-Deane/e/B06XGPG7YZ/ref=sr_tc_2_0?qid=1514742671&sr=1-2-ent

Cliff Dean's Amazon page

https://www.amazon.com/Cliff-Deane/e/B06XGPG7YZ/ref=sr_tc_2_0?qid=1514742671&sr=1-2-ent

VIGILANTE: INTO THE DARKNESS pulls no punches when it comes to the horrific details of a worldwide grid down situation, from the effect on the food chain from ants to rats. With so many dead, how do the survivors deal with rotting corpses, diseases, and villains? Will good triumph over evil? Maybe...

Levi Levins retires from the Army and is off on vacation before starting his new job. He suffers a horrendous loss accompanying "lights out" and must find a way to help humanity to keep his own sanity.

He has no bug out bag, no hidden weapons cache, no transportation, and no Cabin in the woods capable of launching a satellite. What does he do, and how does he do it? Levi will walk us through his path to survival. Perhaps it may one day be yours...

Vigilante: Into the Darkness takes us on a journey to try to stave off the

New Dark Age brought on by a worldwide EMP apocalypse.

Can Government survive when no food is being trucked to the masses? Can our military survive without the tons of food needed each and every meal? The answers are here.

Personally, I can't wait to see how this saga ends.

AJ Newman

*

Books by AJ Newman

American Apocalypse:
American Survivor   Descent Into Darkness (Spring 2018)

Alien Apocalypse: The Virus   Surviving

A Family's Apocalypse Series: Cities on Fire – Family Survival

After the Solar Flare - a Post-Apocalyptic series:
Alone in the Apocalypse   Adventures in the Apocalypse*

The Day America Died series:
New Beginnings   Old Enemies   Frozen Apocalypse

"The Adventures of John Harris" - a Post-Apocalyptic America series:
Surviving   Hell in the Homeland   Tyranny in the Homeland
Revenge in the Homeland...Apocalypse in the Homeland   John Returns

"A Samantha Jones Murder Mystery Thriller series:
Where the Girls Are Buried   Who Killed the Girls?

Books by AJ Newman and Cliff Deane
Terror in the USA: Virus: Strain of Islam

These books are available on Amazon:
http://www.amazon.com/-/e/B00HT84V6U

To contact the Author, please leave comments @:
www.facebook.com/newmananthonyj

About the Author

AJ Newman is the author of 17 science fiction and mystery novels that have been published on Amazon. He was born and raised in a small town in the western part of Kentucky. His Dad taught him how to handle guns very early in life, and he and his best friend Mike spent summers shooting .22 rifles and fishing.

Reading is his passion, and he read every book he could get his hands on and fell in love with science fiction. He graduated from USI with a degree in Chemistry and made a career working in manufacturing and logistics, but always fancied himself as an author.

He served six years in the Army National Guard in an armored unit and spent six years performing every function on M48 and M60 army tanks. This gave him great respect for our veterans who lay their lives on the line to protect our country and freedoms.

He currently resides in a small town just outside of Owensboro, Kentucky with his wife Patsy and their four tiny Shih Tzu's, Sammy, Cotton, Callie, and Benny. All except Benny are rescue dogs.

Made in the USA
Columbia, SC
05 January 2025

49325269R00155